# Step-Chain

All over the country children go to stay with
step-parents, stepbrothers and stepsisters at the
weekends. It's just like an endless chain. A step-
chain. *She's No Angel* is the third link in this step-
chain.

I'm Lissie, and I live with my dad. Usually, I see
Mum and her new family every other weekend,
but now I've got to stay with them for two weeks
because Dad's on holiday. You'd think I'd enjoy
spending time with Mum, but it's a nightmare.
My bratty stepsister is setting me up as a monster
and Mum just won't listen!

Collect the links in the step-chain! You never know who you'll meet on the way...

# SHE'S NO ANGEL

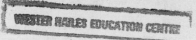
## Ann Bryant

mammoth

# For my great friends Anna and Ole

First published in Great Britain 2001
by Mammoth
an imprint of Egmont Children's Books Limited
a division of Egmont Holding Limited
239 Kensington High Street
London W8 6SA

series editor: Anne Finnis

ISBN 0 7497 4324 7

3 5 7 9 10 8 6 4

Typeset by Avon Dataset Ltd, Bidford on Avon, B50 4JH
(www.avondataset.co.uk)
Printed and bound in Great Britain by
Cox & Wyman Ltd, Reading, Berkshire

# CONTENTS

# Step-Chain

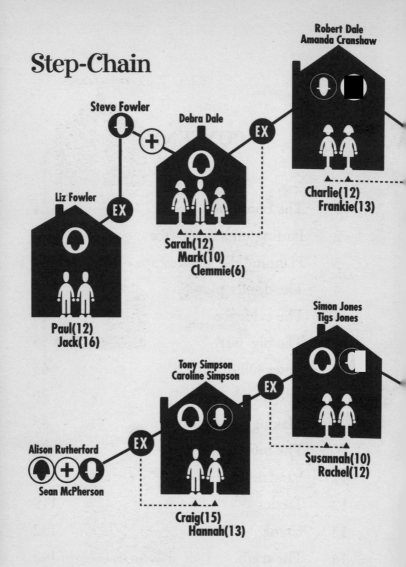

**Robert Dale**
**Amanda Cranshaw**

**Steve Fowler**

**Debra Dale**

**EX**

Charlie(12)
Frankie(13)

**Liz Fowler**

**EX**

Sarah(12)
Mark(10)
Clemmie(6)

Paul(12)
Jack(16)

**Simon Jones**
**Tigs Jones**

**Tony Simpson**
**Caroline Simpson**

**EX**

**Alison Rutherford**

**EX**

**Sean McPherson**

Susannah(10)
Rachel(12)

Craig(15)
Hannah(13)

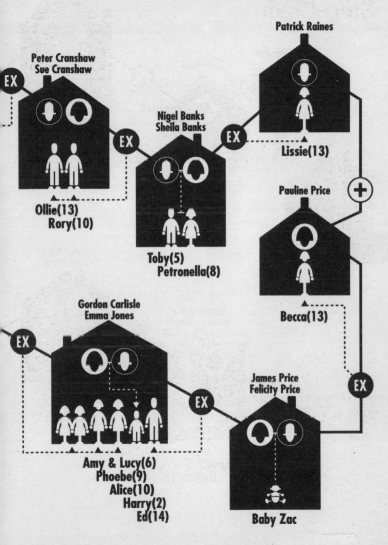

Read on to discover all the links . . .

# 1 THE BOMBSHELL

'Hiya, folks!' said Leanne, chucking her school bag on her desk, which was just across the aisle from mine.

Her three good friends gathered round immediately.

'What have you been up to this weekend, Leanne? You've got that look on your face again!'

Leanne giggled.

I dread this time, first thing Monday morning, when you talk about what you've been doing at the weekend. Today I'd happened to come in at exactly the same time as Leanne, so all the attention would be on her. She's the sort of leader of the group, whereas I'm only on the edge because I'm not as good at making friends. Everyone always gathers round Leanne, and right now she was looking as though she was about to report something really interesting. With any luck I might escape the Monday morning interrogation.

'I went to London!' she announced, looking round proudly.

Gasps went up.

'How come you never told us on Friday?' asked Donna.

Leanne suddenly let out her breath and pulled a face as she spoke slowly. 'Because it was nothing great. It was my brother's graduation ceremony, and though Mum and Dad were in seventh heaven for the entire weekend, I was actually so bored I counted the bricks in the wall behind the stage!'

Everyone laughed. Leanne always makes people want to talk to her and laugh with her. I wish I could do that. Even when she's had a boring weekend, she's still swinging along happily.

'I went to my cousin's birthday party on Saturday night and it was fantastic!' said Donna.

'You lucky thing!' said Leanne, pouting and pretending she was jealous.

'I danced for three solid hours! The music was brilliant!'

'Yeah, and Donna and I went shopping in that new shopping centre,' said Jo. 'Mum was in a really good mood. She gave me an advance on my allowance and I bought those black trousers I wanted *and* that pink top!'

I pretended to be looking in my school bag,

and started silently chanting my usual prayer for every other Monday morning: *Please don't ask me what I've been doing.* I can't bear it when they all look at me as though they feel sorry for me, so recently I've started pretending I've had a great time at my mum's. I'm not sure they're convinced though, and that makes it even worse. They probably talk about me afterwards behind my back.

'What did you do, Gemma?'

I breathed out. I was off the hook again.

'My aunt and uncle came for the weekend.'

'Cool! The uncle who works at Channel 4?'

'Yeah. He told us some great stories.'

I couldn't scrabble around in my bag forever and as I glanced up I saw Leanne looking at me. Uh-oh! Here we go.

'What did *you* do, Lissie?'

I frowned at my nails then began to gnaw at one of them. I was getting very good at appearing unconcerned when inside I was completely churned up.

'Oh, nothing much . . .'

'Was it your weekend to go to your mum's?'

'Yeah.'

There was a pause and I could feel everyone's eyes on me. They were waiting for me to say something else, but how could I tell them what had really happened?

*We went to Toby and Petronella's school fête on Saturday afternoon, where they both got to do and buy just about everything they wanted, and when they didn't win the games, they sulked. On Sunday morning I practised my cello which wasn't easy, because my half-sister was deliberately playing her music loudly in her bedroom.*

I didn't say anything.

'What did you do on Saturday? Anything good?'

This was it. Either I had to tell the truth and

admit that I'd had a totally terrible time because I couldn't stand my eight-year-old half-sister and my five-year-old half-brother, or I had to tell the usual lie and pretend that I'd had a great time. But I felt so pathetic admitting that I'd had another miserable weekend. It made me look stupid for not doing something about it. And I knew I *was* stupid. It was just so much easier to suffer in silence. After all, it was only two little days out of every fourteen – or even sometimes only one. And they *were* my half-sister and -brother.

'Nothing much . . .' I quickly changed the subject. 'Has anyone got any nail polish remover on them?'

I didn't miss the look that passed between Donna and Leanne. I bet they were thinking, *Fancy putting up with spending every other weekend with two children you can't stick. How sad is that?*

* * *

It was a quarter past six when Dad got home. Gemma's mum had just dropped me back from music club, as she did every Monday.

'Hi, Liss,' Dad said to me, as he started opening the mail. 'How was school?'

'Fine.'

I was sure he wasn't concentrating on me at all.

'We had choir practice at lunchtime.'

'Uh-huh.'

He screwed up the contents of the envelope, made a ball out of it and aimed it at the bin, before opening the next envelope.

'And I got C minus for that biology homework that you helped me with. So thanks very much, Dad.'

'Uh-huh.'

He was scanning through a phone bill, a frown on his face.

'We had some visitors at school this afternoon.'

'Uh-huh.'

Right, Dad, let's see if you're really listening.

'Yeah. Some gorillas. They just strolled in and started taking over from the teachers.'

'Uh-huh.'

'One of them was called Goliath, and I hope you don't mind but I liked him so much that I've signed the adoption papers and he's up in my bedroom watching television with a banana and a bag of cheese and onion crisps.'

Dad stopped reading and gave me a vague sort of smile. 'That's great,' he said. 'Sorry – who did you say was upstairs?'

'You weren't listening to a single word I said, Dad.'

'Yes I was!' he protested. 'I just didn't hear who you said was in your room.'

'Goliath the gorilla!' I informed him, with a

withering look, to show him just how hopeless he was.

He looked a bit embarrassed then. 'Sorry, Liss. Has my black shirt come out of the wash?'

'I think so. Why? Are you going out?'

'Yes, in about an hour, I'm going to . . .'

He broke off and sat down at the table. Suddenly I knew that he was about to say something important. Half a dozen possibilities flashed through my mind. Maybe he and Pauline had had a big row and Dad had found himself a new girlfriend. That would be terrible because I really like Pauline. Dad's only been going out with her for about a month, but he seems so happy. I'd hate it if they broke up. She isn't the first girlfriend Dad's had since he and Mum split up all those years ago, but even though I've only met her a few times I've got a feeling she's something special, and that Dad thinks so too.

Maybe he's taking her out for dinner and he's going to propose to her. That would be great! I'd get to be a bridesmaid. Then she could come and live in this house and I'd feel like I was in a proper family again . . . OK, I knew I was only building castles in the air, because you don't usually get married when you've only known someone a month.

Dad was looking at me carefully. 'The thing is, Liss . . . Pauline and I . . .' My heart hammered, '. . . are going away together. Someone at work has got a place in Portugal, and we're going to rent it. So this evening we're meeting this chap and his wife to sort out the details.'

It was weird. It was like a bombshell without an explosion. I couldn't work out what the big deal was. It was great that Dad and Pauline had decided to have a holiday together. Maybe that would make them want to live together all the time. So why was my heart still banging away?

With Dad's next words I suddenly knew.

'You'll be staying at Mum's, Liss.'

He was giving me one of those encouraging smiles that you give little kids when you're telling them what fun it is at the dentist's.

I didn't want him to feel guilty about going away with Pauline, because Dad hardly ever does anything except work, so I tried to sound unfazed.

'How long for?'

Please let it only be a week!

'A fortnight.'

My heart stopped hammering and plummeted to my toes.

# 2 PUTTING ON A BRAVE FACE

It was Saturday morning and Dad and I were standing in the middle of the kitchen surrounded by bags and cases and, most important of all, my cello case. I've been playing the cello for four years and it's my very favourite thing in the world. I have my cello lesson every Thursday after school and Mrs Martin, my teacher, enters me for festivals and exams.

'Now don't forget, I want you on that stage next Wednesday, playing your heart out. I shall be there in spirit, if not in the flesh,' said Dad, giving me a big smile.

Dad was talking about the final of the inter-house music competition, which was one of the biggest events on the school calendar. The school hall was always packed out for the final. This was the first year I'd been able to enter for it, because last year I was too young. It's usually the Year Elevens and the sixth-formers who get through to the final, and I'm only Year Eight so I don't suppose I stand any chance.

'I'll never make it to the final. There are loads of good musicians higher up the school, you know, and you have to get through two heats to get into the final. There are only four finalists altogether – one from each house. Anyway, Harriet Sherborne's in my house and she's a really good violinist, *and* she's in Year Twelve. So don't hold your breath, Dad.'

'Who decides who goes through to the finals?'

'Mr Crane, the school music teacher. He's only heard me play in the school orchestra though. He's never actually heard me playing one of my pieces solo or anything.'

'Why not? You shouldn't hide your light under a bushel all the time, Liss.'

'It'd be showing off, Dad. I couldn't go marching up to him and say, "*Oh Mr Crane I really think you ought to hear how good I am on the cello. Let me play you one of my pieces.*"'

Dad knitted his eyebrows together then broke into a smile.

'Well, now's your chance to show him your stuff. When do the heats take place?'

'The Year Elevens and the sixth-formers have already done theirs. The younger ones like me have to play to him on Monday lunchtime. I reckon he's already decided who's going through, though. He'd never choose a little Year Eight, Dad.'

I didn't want to get Dad's hopes up – and, more importantly, I didn't want to get *mine* up, because I'd be so disappointed if I didn't get through. All the same, there was a little part of me which secretly thought I might be in with the teeniest of chances if I played really well to Mr Crane.

'There's always a first time, Liss. I bet you'll get through both heats and finish up playing in the final. And you'll have your mum and Nigel there to whistle and clap and stamp and cheer you on!'

'It's not a race, Dad!'

He looked at his watch. 'No, but *this* is! Come on, I don't want to miss my plane. We need to allow twenty-five minutes to get to Mum's.'

The moment had finally arrived when I had

to say goodbye. I was dreading the thought of having to put up with my spoilt little half-brother and -sister for two whole weeks, when I can hardly bear them for two hours, but I was going to have to put on a brave face for Dad's sake. I'd never told him just how much I hated the Saturdays I spent at Mum's. It was bad enough being so far away from my friends, because it took nearly half an hour to get to Mum's, but then there was the problem of my half-sister and -brother. Dad knew I wasn't exactly bowled over by Petronella and Toby, but he'd be upset if he knew just how bad things were.

The trouble is I don't want to make problems between Mum and Dad. Even though I was only little when they split up, I can still remember all the arguing and shouting that went on. It didn't stop after they'd split up either. I dreaded it every time they talked to each other or even when the phone rang. They couldn't have a conversation for more than thirty seconds without it turning into a row. The raised voices and hateful looks were really scary. Things have gradually got better over the years, and now they can even manage to talk normally and politely to each other. The big change came when Dad met Pauline. It was as though he finally got over Mum leaving him. That's why I'm not about to stir things up again.

I used to live with Mum when my parents first split up, but spent more and more time with Dad because Mum always seemed so busy with Petronella when she was tiny, and even busier when Toby was born. In the end I started living permanently with Dad, and went to Mum and Nigel's at weekends, then gradually that got changed to every other weekend.

Some weekends at Mum's are better than others. It depends how much I have to cross the little brats' paths. Of course I love my mum, but it's kind of different from the way I love Dad. I know it's strange, but I still feel like a bit of a visitor when I go to Mum and Nigel's. It's not at all like a second home: it's as though Mum's got her new family, all tucked in round the edges, and I'm a bit of an extra. She and Nigel are very nice to me, but I can't ever relax properly and say exactly what I want. Probably a good thing really, or I might say something I'd regret about Petronella and Toby.

I can't stick those kids at any price because they're so spoilt. What's more, they can't stick me. Don't ask me why. I haven't a clue. Maybe they don't like sharing their house and their parents with me – even though one of their parents happens to be one of mine.

'She's here!' came a shrill scream from Petronella as I got out of the car.

She was standing just inside the front door and it sounded like she was addressing the Pyramids, the way her voice carried. Toby didn't appear, thank goodness. With any luck he'd gone to play at a friend's or something.

'Hello, darling!' said Mum, coming out to meet me and picking up one of the bags. She looked as though she'd been crying. 'Sorry, I've been cooking onions. Lots of them. We've got a few friends coming over this evening. And I'm making lasagne for lunch, so I hope you're hungry.'

I managed a brave smile as I kissed Dad goodbye and told him to have a great time.

He hugged me and called out to Mum, 'Everything OK?'

'Yes. Have a good time. Sorry, mustn't let

the onions burn.' And with that, she rushed back inside.

'Phone you this evening when we're there, Liss. 'Bye.'

He looked quite sad as he got back in his car. I think he was suddenly feeling sorry for me, so I waved him right out of sight with a big bright smile on my face just in case he could still see me in his mirror.

When I turned round Petronella was still standing there.

'It's lasagne for lunch.'

'Good, I love lasagne. Here, can you take one of these bags, Petronella?'

'I'm not allowed to carry heavy things. I've hurt my wrist.'

'Take this small one then. It's not heavy.'

'I'm not supposed to carry anything really.'

At that point Mum reappeared. 'Come on, Petronella. Let's help Lissie with her bags. We can't have her struggling.'

'What about my wrist? It's really hurting, you know.'

'Is it, darling? Don't worry then. I expect we can manage between the two of us.'

As Mum picked up the heaviest bag, Petronella gave me a sly look as if to say, *See! I don't have to do what you say.* She followed us upstairs, and I was surprised because Mum was making for Petronella's bedroom. I usually sleep in Toby's room and he moves into Petronella's.

'We thought it might be nice for you to have a bit of company, Lissie,' said Mum, sounding rather unsure of herself. I glanced at Petronella. She was wearing that smug look again and I knew she'd had something to do with this decision.

'I'm fine in Toby's room, honestly,' I tried. But I knew, even as I was saying it, that

Petronella would get her own way.

'I'm too old to share with a boy,' she told me importantly.

'We thought it was easier than moving Toby out, you see,' Mum explained. 'It's all right at the weekend, but for a whole fortnight, it's less disruptive.'

She made me feel as though I was being a nuisance, just by being there. I knew I'd hate sharing with Petronella for two whole weeks, but it looked as though I didn't have any choice. As usual at Mum's, I just had to keep quiet and put up with it.

'Petronella will show you where you can put your clothes. She's cleared a bit of space, haven't you, Pepsi?'

Petronella lifted her chin up as though she was about to nod, but it stayed up in the air when Mum went back down to get on with the cooking.

'The reason we're having lasagne for lunch is because *you're* here,' she informed me in an unfriendly tone of voice.

'That's nice,' I said, trying not to sound sarcastic.

'It's only for today,' she went on. 'Tomorrow we'll go back to eating things that Toby and me like.'

I took a deep breath, counted to ten, then said, 'Just show me which drawers are for me and I'll unpack, Petronella.'

'The bottom two,' she said, then she flounced out and I flopped back on the bed and stared at the cciling. It looked as though this fortnight was going to be every bit as bad as my worst nightmare.

# 3 PLANNING THE
# GREAT ESCAPE

A moment later I suddenly had the feeling that someone was watching me. I lay perfectly still and listened hard. The smallest of stifled giggles sounded outside the half-open door. I guessed Toby must have been hiding and now he was spying on me through the crack in the back of the door. Right, I'd soon put a stop to that. Pretending I hadn't noticed, I got up calmly and went over to shut the door, but I'd only moved it a few centimetres when there came an ear-piercing scream from the other side of it. I opened it quickly to see Toby standing there clutching his finger, tears streaming down his face.

'You trapped my finger in the door, you did!' he was wailing loudly. 'I'm telling my daddy when he gets back from football.'

Mum came rushing upstairs and Toby threw himself at her. 'She trapped my finger. She did it on purpose.'

'I didn't,' I said softly to Mum.

She was holding Toby close and examining his finger. The nail and the whole top joint of his index finger were very red.

'Ssh, ssh, ssh,' Mum said. 'Let's put it under the cold tap, darling. Then it won't hurt so much.'

'She trapped it,' Toby repeated, pointing the finger at me before sticking it in his mouth and eyeing me warily as though I couldn't be trusted not to do some more damage if I wasn't watched carefully.

'I didn't know he was behind the door, Mum,' I told her.

Petronella suddenly appeared. 'Toby was waiting for Lissie to say whether he could come in,' she said with a sly look on her face. 'You knocked, didn't you, Toby?'

'Yes,' said Toby, with a slightly bewildered look on his face.

'I never heard a knock,' I said, knowing that Petronella had made that up on the spur of the moment.

'He *did* knock, Mum. Didn't you, Toby?'

'Look, let's forget about it,' said Mum. 'It was just an accident. You two come downstairs now and let Lissie get on with her unpacking.'

'I want to go in *my* room,' said Petronella.

'You don't have to go in right this minute, do you?' asked Mum a bit impatiently.

'It's OK, I'll unpack later,' I said, almost

knocking Mum over as I dived past her to go downstairs, I was so desperate to get away.

'Hello Pepsie! Hello Tobes!' said Nigel, coming into the living-room later.

'Say hello to Lissie, Daddy!' Toby shouted. (He was *so* loud. Was I the only one who seemed to think so? Maybe the others had just got used to it.) 'You've been playing football, haven't you, Daddy?'

'Oh hello, Lissie,' Nigel said. 'Sorry, I didn't see you there. I hope these two little rascals are behaving themselves.'

*No, they're being complete pains in the bum!*

I smiled vaguely, but he didn't see. He was too busy laughing as he fended off the 'little rascals', who had pulled him to the ground and were jumping on his back, playing horses.

'I don't know how you're going to put up with this madhouse for two weeks, Lissie!' said

Nigel, struggling to stand up while Toby clung to his back. He tried to shake Toby off, but Toby had got hold of his shirt and wasn't letting go.

'Let go, Toby, you'll tear it,' said Nigel.

But Toby just laughed and called out at the top of his voice, 'I'm a baby koala so I cling to my daddy's back.'

Petronella was skipping wildly round and round her dad, while I just sat on one end of the settee feeling like an audience of one at the circus.

'Come on, you monsters,' said Mum, coming into the room and smiling at all the fun. 'Daddy's tired from his football and Simon and Sally and the others will be here soon.'

Mum had spent most of the afternoon in the kitchen cooking for their friends that evening. I'd been into town to spend my pocket money then gone back to Mum's and played on the computer, but I'd only been on it for about ten minutes when Petronella had come in and taken over.

'Right, that really is enough,' said Nigel, putting on his strictest voice, which wouldn't scare a fly.

'Come on, Daddy Koala, take me for a walk!' cried Toby, still clutching hold of Nigel's shirt while kicking him in his sides to try and get him to move. It looked really painful. I don't know why Nigel put up with it.

'Yes, come on, Daddy Koala,' said Petronella, who was just as excited. 'Let me help you on your way.' And she began pushing Nigel's bottom.

And just then there was a ripping noise.

'Now look what you've done,' said Mum, looking very cross as she unpeeled Toby and put him down on the carpet, where he sat scowling and red. Petronella went and sat on the settee. Mum kept going with the telling-off, but her voice wasn't sounding quite so cross any more. 'Daddy's shirt is all torn! You were told to get down, Toby, and that's what happens when you don't do as you're told.'

Neither Toby nor Petronella made a sound. They just sat there.

'I'll go and change,' said Nigel.

Mum came and sat down with me. 'Thank goodness for *one* quiet one,' she said.

'I'm quiet too, Mummy,' said Petronella. 'Look at me.'

She was sitting up very straight with her mouth pursed and her eyes all big and innocent.

'Yes, well done, darling,' said Mum, before turning back to me. 'Lissie, would you like to earn some money this evening? You can say no if you want.'

'What doing?' I asked, feeling a bit excited, because anything that would get me out of having to spend a single minute with my half-brother and -sister would be good.

'I wondered if you'd like to help serve and wash up this evening. There'll be eight of us altogether.'

'Yes, I'd love to.'

'Can I help too?' asked Petronella.

'You can help for a bit, darling, but I want you in bed by nine at the latest.'

'Aww! That means I'll hardly get to see Uncle Clive and Auntie Jan,' moaned Petronella.

'Everyone'll be here at eight, so you'll see them for an hour,' said Mum. 'Lissie, let me show you the new cafetière.'

I followed her out of the sitting-room and – surprise, surprise – the others came too.

'This is the cafetière,' said Petronella, pushing past Mum and grabbing it. 'And if you want to know where anything else is kept, just ask me, all right?'

'I do actually know where most things are kept,' I told her, trying not to let my irritation show too much.

'Why don't you go and play with Toby, Petronella?' asked Mum with a bright smile, before turning back to show me the puddings in the freezer.

Petronella sat down at the table, but Mum didn't seem to notice.

'The cheese can go on this special plate and I've got some butter which can go into a little dish instead of marge,' went on Mum. 'Oh, and the clingfilm is in that drawer. If you transfer the leftovers from the big serving dishes into smaller dishes in that cupboard, you can cover them with clingfilm and put them in the fridge.'

'OK,' I said.

'Lissie won't be able to remember all that, Mummy,' said Petronella.

'Yes, she will. She's a bright girl with a good memory,' said Mum, which made me feel very proud.

'My memory's *really* good, isn't it, Mummy? Remember what Mrs Hartley said in my report?'

'Yes, darling, of course I remember.'

'So by the time I'm Lissie's age, my memory'll probably be better than hers, won't it?'

I could tell Mum wasn't really listening. Her mind was on the meal. 'Yes, I expect so . . .'

I would have liked to wipe the smug look off Petronella's face and tell her to stop having to be the most important person all the time, but I didn't want to make waves, so I kept quiet.

When Mum had shown me everything, she took Toby upstairs with her so he could get ready for bed then come down in his dressing-gown. Nigel came down then, and started opening wine while I sorted out the plates and dishes. A few minutes later we went into the dining-room and Petronella followed.

'Do you want serviettes, Nigel?' I asked.

'Good thinking,' he said.

'I'll get them. I know which ones,' said Petronella, making a dive for the sideboard.

'What about salt and pepper?' I asked.

'Right again!' said Nigel with a smile.

'Mummy and Daddy use the tall silver ones for dinner parties,' said Petronella. 'I'll get them. You don't know where they are.'

'Shall I put the nuts and crisps and things in little dishes in the sitting-room, Nigel?' I asked, trying to ignore Petronella. 'It's nearly eight o'clock.'

'What would we do without you, Lissie,' he said, patting me on the back, which I took to be a 'yes'.

Petronella pushed in front of me. 'You don't know which dishes we use,' she said as she pelted through to the kitchen.

'I'm sure you're going to be a manageress one day, Pepsi,' said Nigel, smiling away at his bossy little daughter.

In the kitchen I found that she'd ripped open the bag of pistachio nuts a bit too forcefully and sent them shooting all over the floor.

'Oh, *you* do it,' she said grumpily as she went marching out. I felt a bit like Cinderella all of a sudden.

As I was sweeping them into the dustpan, Mum came in. 'Oh dear . . . never mind, Lissie. We've got loads of other nuts, don't worry.'

'It wasn't . . .'

Oh, what was the point! Something told me that the evening wasn't going to be such a great escape from the little brats, after all.

# 4 THE DINNER PARTY

At ten-past eight the first guests arrived.

'Come and say hello,' said Mum, and I followed her into the hall.

Four people had arrived together. Toby launched himself at one of the men, who scooped him up and pretended to eat him.

'Get off, Uncle Clive,' screeched Toby. 'You're hurting.'

'Lovely! Roast boy! Excellent dinner, Sheila,' said Clive to Mum. I didn't know him from Adam. He wasn't a proper uncle.

'Eat me instead!' cried Petronella, jumping up and down at his feet.

'Fried girl! Yum!' said Clive. Then his wife suddenly noticed me.

'Hello, you must be Lissie. I'm Jan and this is Clive, if you hadn't guessed.'

She was rolling her eyes at the ceiling. I liked her.

'Lissie's daddy has gone away on holiday with his girlfriend,' said Petronella loudly.

'That's nice,' said Jan, but everyone looked a bit embarrassed.

'This is Simon and Sally,' said Nigel quickly, introducing the other couple, who seemed very quiet.

They both said hello and then Nigel took all the coats.

'Shall I put them upstairs?' I asked.

'I'll take them,' said Petronella. 'I know where they go.'

The guests went through to the sitting-room with Mum and Nigel and I watched Petronella struggling upstairs with the coats.

'Can you manage?' I asked her. 'Do you want me to help you?'

'I'm OK,' she snapped back, so I headed for the kitchen, but I'd hardly taken two steps when she called out, 'OK, *you* can do it. They're too heavy for me.'

She came skipping downstairs and went straight into the sitting-room. She'd left all the coats in a heap halfway up the stairs. I picked them up and put them on Mum and Nigel's bed. One of them was a beautiful cream coat, but as I laid it on the bed, I noticed the lining had got a big rip in it. I thought it was Sally's. It seemed odd that she'd come out with it like that, when everything else about Sally was so neat and smart.

When I went back into the kitchen

Petronella was standing there, holding Toby's hand. There was something different about her. She looked guilty. Her eyes were big and she had two bright red spots on her cheeks.

'Mummy says can you put Toby to bed, Lissie?' she said.

'Are you all right?' I asked her.

She nodded and turned away.

When Toby and I were at the top of the stairs we heard the doorbell ring. Toby was all for running back down and answering it, but I tightened my grip on his hand and said, 'Come on. Mummy said bedtime.'

'Mummy always reads me a story and stays with me till I fall asleep.'

'I'll read you a story, but I'm not staying with you till you fall asleep because I've got lots to do in the kitchen. You're a big boy now. You can think about the story after I've gone and that will send you to sleep.'

I picked the shortest story in the book and as I read it, Toby sucked his thumb noisily. Amazing! I thought. He even sucks his thumb loudly. He was asleep by the end of the story, so I crept out.

The moment I was back in the kitchen Petronella came in and said, 'Mum wants a little bowl of soured cream and a teaspoon. It's to go into the soup.'

I opened the cupboard where I knew Mum kept the lovely white china gravy boat that goes with the rest of the dinner service, but it wasn't there.

'No, she usually uses the little jug with flowers on it,' Petronella informed me.

'What, even for guests?'

She nodded. Why wasn't I convinced?

I filled the flowery jug with soured cream from the fridge and was about to carry it through, when Petronella grabbed it from me. 'I'll take it.'

'Mind you don't spill it!' I called, as she charged off at a hundred miles an hour.

I gave the soup a stir then switched on the TV. It was 8.40. Only twenty minutes to go till Madam's bedtime.

'Right,' said Mum, coming into the kitchen like a whirlwind. 'Let's get the soup on the table.'

She tipped it from the pan into a big tureen while I got some lovely Italian bread out of the oven, sliced it, and put the pieces in the bread basket.

'That looks perfect, Lissie.'

All the guests were watching Petronella, who was standing on a chair holding an imaginary microphone and singing a song about a crocodile in a loud, tuneless voice. Nigel was smiling at her as though she was his favourite pop star. Even Mum stopped in her tracks, eyes shining with pride.

Petronella really had got the pair of them wrapped around her little finger, but the other men were getting fidgety. In fact, Simon was trying to stifle a yawn. The women were smiling but I wasn't sure whether they were faking it or not. It was quite a relief when Petronella finally shut up and everyone clapped. Mum put the soup on the table.

'Mmm! Smells lovely!' said Jan, as Mum took the lid off.

I put the bread down beside it and Mum introduced me to the other two guests. Maria asked me lots of questions about where I went to school and what my hobbies were. I kept on wishing she'd stop, because I always think grown-ups are just being polite when they ask you questions. And when she asked me what grade I was on at cello, I felt as though I was showing off when I said seven.

'Did you hear that, Patrick? Lissie's on grade

seven cello. That's excellent, isn't it?'

Everyone was nodding and congratulating me and I knew I was going red. I was desperate to get back to the kitchen.

Petronella was trying to get Jan and Clive to watch her imitating Irish dancing. It was obvious they were wishing she'd just go away, because they only looked at her for about ten seconds then turned to the people sitting opposite them and started making conversation.

'Come and help in the kitchen, Petronella,' I said.

'You *are* lucky, having such a helpful daughter around, Sheila,' said Sally, smiling at me.

Petronella looked furious. 'I've been helping too, haven't I, Mummy?'

'Yes darling,' said Mum. And just then the door opened and in came a very sleepy-looking Toby.

'I woke up,' he said, going straight over to Mum and trying to pull at the back of her chair.

'Oh dear, Tobes,' said Mum, pushing her chair back and taking Toby on her lap. 'Did you have a bad dream?'

There was a short pause then Toby said, 'Yes – about pirates.'

'*My* little boy will be fast asleep in bed by now,' said Maria to Toby.

'Well he's not *me,* is he?' Toby replied, staring at her with big hostile eyes from the safety of Mum's lap, his thumb wedged firmly in his mouth.

I waited for Mum or Nigel to tell Toby off for being cheeky . . .

'He's got an answer for everything,' Nigel said proudly to Simon.

As soon as Nigel turned back to Toby I saw Simon and Sally give each other a look.

'Do you want me to take Toby up, Mum?' I asked her quietly. 'I'll read him another story.'

'Do you want to go up with Lissie?' Mum asked him in a soppy voice. Toby buried his head and snuggled even closer to her.

'Don't worry, Lissie,' said Mum. 'I'll take him up in a minute.'

Mum then tried to eat her soup without spilling any on Toby's head. I could see the guests thought Toby and Petronella were spoilt and it made me feel ashamed.

'Coming, Petronella?' I tried again.

'In a minute,' she replied.

I give up!

# 5 THE EVIDENCE

Mum and I carried the main course in together and all the guests said how lovely it smelt and looked. Petronella was dancing round the table. I glanced at my watch and saw that it was after nine. Mum must have noticed me looking.

'Right! Bedtime, young lady,' she said.

'I'm not going up if Toby's still down here,' said Petronella. 'I'm older than him so I can stay up later.'

Mum tried to unpeel Toby from Nigel.

'Come on, Tobes. Up we go to beddy-byes.'

'I want to sleep on Daddy,' said Toby.

Mum tried pulling, but he was clinging like a leech. As I went back to the kitchen for the rest of the vegetables I heard Sally say, 'Come on, Toby, leave your poor daddy alone.' When I came back a minute later, Petronella was trying to yank Toby off Nigel's knee with all her might, while Nigel was telling her to let go. She wasn't taking any notice of him whatsoever. Mum spoke a bit more sharply.

'Just leave him, Petronella. Daddy and I will sort it out. It would be a great help if you could just go to bed.'

Petronella let go and went out without a word. I couldn't believe it.

'Come on, Tobes,' Mum tried again in a pleading tone. 'Come up with Mummy now.'

But Toby was practically crawling inside

Nigel's shirt he was so determined not to go to bed.

'Why don't you take him up, Nigel?' said Jan, sounding a bit irritated.

Nigel looked rather taken aback, but then he got up and headed for the door, saying that he'd be back in a minute. Immediately Toby jumped down and ran to Mum, crying and shouting and protesting like a two-year-old. And unbelievably, Mum picked him up and started cuddling him. I saw Maria's husband close his eyes slowly as though he couldn't believe what he was seeing. Even Jan was pursing her lips.

Suddenly I couldn't bear it any longer. I just wanted to get Toby out of there, so that the grown-ups could go back to how they were – all smiley and chatty.

'Come on, Toby. You won't be allowed any of the leftover chocolate pudding for lunch tomorrow if you don't do as you're told.'

He stopped crying and looked at me in amazement. There was a silence as though I'd stunned everyone. All eyes were on me, and I knew I was going red again. The moment I saw Toby relaxing his grip on Nigel I pulled him down by grabbing his hand, which tipped him off balance. Then I flung open the door, still gripping his hand tightly, and said, 'Race you! One two three go!'

He shot out of the door like an arrow and I kept just behind him all the way upstairs and into his room. It was a big relief that Toby had acted how I'd hoped he would *and* I was well away from those watching eyes.

Once he was in bed, I started to make up a story about a little boy called Toby who won the race to bed. I'd got his attention by then and it was easy to make my voice go softer and softer until I saw his eyes beginning to close.

Unfortunately the phone rang and made them fly open again. Someone answered it after only two rings so I carried on talking in my soft voice for another five minutes, until I was quite certain he was fast asleep, then I crept out and pulled his door to.

I was about to go downstairs when I suddenly remembered Petronella's quick exit earlier on. I put my head round her bedroom door (*our* bedroom door), expecting to see her in bed, but the bed was empty. I went to the bathroom. That was empty too. I looked in every room upstairs then came down and searched everywhere except the dining-room. Petronella was nowhere to be seen.

I sat at the kitchen table and thought what to do. Part of me reckoned I should rush into Mum and Nigel and tell them that Petronella had disappeared. But there was another little voice in my head insisting that she wouldn't have gone out in the cold and the dark, and it would have been impossible for an intruder to get in and take her away without making some sort of noise. Then I thought back to the way she'd left the dining-room so quickly and quietly when Mum asked her, for the second time, to go to bed. I wondered if she'd gone back in there. I *bet* she had.

I opened the door quietly. Petronella was curled up in the corner of the room lying on four cushions from the sitting-room. She gave me a smug look as if to say, *See! I don't have to do anything I don't want to do,* then she closed her eyes and pretended to be fast asleep. Mum and Nigel must have been out of their tiny minds letting her stay there! She always got what she wanted because neither one of them was strong enough to stand up to her.

All the grown-ups were laughing and chatting. At least they'd forgotten about

Petronella. I bet she was dying for me to tell her to go to bed and for Mum to say, *Leave her alone, Lissie, she's not doing any harm over there in the corner.* Well, I wouldn't give her the satisfaction. I ignored her and turned to Mum.

'Just wondering if you needed anything else, Mum?'

'Could you bring another bottle of white wine from the fridge?' Nigel asked me.

I went back into the kitchen, got the wine, and was about to return to the dining-room when something caught my eye under the table. It was a tiny piece of bone china. I picked it up, and as I stared at it in the palm of my hand, it slowly dawned on me what it was. Petronella must have broken the gravy boat. I couldn't help it, my mind went rushing forwards. She wasn't going to own up about it – or worse, she was going to try and pin the blame on me!

The bin was by the boiler. My heart was beating fast as I lifted the lid. There was no obvious sign of broken china, but Petronella was cunning. She might have buried it. I tipped the bin slightly so the kitchen light was shining right into it. There was no way there was any broken china in there, because the bin was practically empty.

*You're getting paranoid, Melissa!*

The piece of china couldn't have been the gravy boat after all. I gave myself a sharp talking to, then returned to the dining-room with the wine, hardly giving Sleeping Beauty a glance.

It was later, when I was putting the pudding dishes into the dishwasher and feeling quite tired, that I suddenly had another thought. I went out of the back door and round the side of the house to the big wheelie bin. Flipping the lid back I untied the top bin liner. There was a bit of light from the lamp at the front corner of the house but I couldn't really see much at all, so I wheeled the bin over to it and peered inside.

There, nestling amongst the orange peel and prawn shells, were four pieces of broken white china. One of them was the handle to the gravy boat. As I stared into the bin I remembered that look of guilt on Petronella's face when she'd asked me to put Toby to bed. Now I understood.

# 6 THE BIG 'BUT'

One thing I really like at Mum's is Sunday breakfast. We always have bacon and eggs, sausage and tomato. And without fail, Mum always makes some comment like, *We shouldn't be eating this, really. It's not very good for us at all,* or *I wonder how many calories in this lot? I'll have to be really sensible for the rest of the day.*

On this particular Sunday we all tucked into our lovely bad-for-you meal, and I kept waiting for Mum to make one of her usual comments, but she never did. In fact she didn't talk at all, and when I looked at her face I thought she looked anxious about something. Nigel wasn't exactly chatty either. I wondered if they'd both had too much to drink last night and now they'd got hangovers. I glanced from one to the other and suddenly knew that it was more than that. Something was wrong. Petronella was being unusually quiet too. If Toby hadn't been there the silence would have been awful.

Toby, of course, didn't know the meaning of quiet. He was telling us a long story about something that had happened at school. I wasn't listening properly and it was obvious Mum wasn't either. She was staring into space, miles away. Petronella kept casting sideways looks at her. I wished I could read minds at that moment.

'You did a very good job last night, Lissie,' Mum suddenly said to me.

'I was telling you about Jamie Harding actually,' said Toby.

Everybody ignored him.

'Yes, very good indeed,' added Nigel.

Why did I get the feeling there was more to come? It was like there was a big 'but' just over the horizon.

'I must remember to pay you,' went on Mum.

I smiled and reached for some toast, still waiting.

'Listen to me again now,' Toby said loudly.

Nobody took any notice.

'Maria's nice, isn't she?' I commented, as I spread butter on my toast.

Mum seemed delighted that I'd said something. 'Yes, she's lovely. And what did you think of Sally?'

The question took me aback.

'Er . . . very nice, yes.'

Mum suddenly put her knife and fork together and gave me a very serious look.

'When Sally came to go, Lissie, she found that the lining of her coat was all ripped.'

So *that* was what this was all about. I should have guessed. 'It was ripped when I put it on your bed, Mum. I thought at the time it was weird that she'd wear it like that.'

There was a short silence. Mum looked at her plate. Nigel got up and went over to the kettle.

'Do you want *me* to make the tea?' asked Petronella, all sweetness and light.

I glanced at her smug face and knew precisely what had happened. The memory of Petronella struggling clumsily upstairs with the coats was still very clear in my mind. She'd got practically to the top of the stairs when she'd changed her mind for no real reason and left them all there in a heap for me to take to the bedroom. It was so obvious what must have happened. She'd trodden on the bottom of Sally's coat, ripped the lining and decided not to own up. And Mum thought I'd done it. She'd been hoping I'd own up. And right now she was looking at me as though she didn't believe a word I was saying.

'I'm afraid that coat was *not* torn at the beginning of the evening, Lissie. Sally was clearly very upset when she saw it. She tried not to make a fuss about it, but I bet she was secretly furious. I felt so ashamed that it had happened in this house.'

'Well, I'm sorry, Mum, but it wasn't me.' I looked pointedly at Petronella, who was looking intently at the kettle. 'It was ripped when I put it on the bed . . . Why don't you ask Petronella about it? She was the one who insisted on carrying the coats upstairs even though they were dragging under her feet half the time.'

'It wasn't me. Why do you have to blame me?' Petronella suddenly exploded dramatically. 'You're just trying to get me into trouble.'

Suddenly I'd had enough of my cunning little half-sister.

'Well, you're the one who broke the gravy boat and didn't own up about it, aren't you?' I shot back at her.

There was a silence. Mum looked suitably shocked. Good! About time she realised that her precious little Pepsi wasn't quite so wonderful as she seemed. Petronella didn't say a word, which surprised me. I thought she'd at least try to protest her innocence. Mum spoke in a cold, quiet voice.

'Petronella *has* owned up about the gravy boat, actually, Melissa.'

It was my turn to look shocked. This was the last thing I'd expected. I glanced at Petronella, who was pouring milk into the mugs.

'I always own up when I've done something wrong, don't I, Mummy?' she said in a sugary voice that made me sick.

'Yes, you usually do,' said Mum, giving me a *Now what have you got to say for yourself?* look.

I felt terrible. Not only did Mum think I'd ripped her friend's coat, kept it a secret, and told a lie about it. She also thought I'd tried to get Petronella into trouble about it, and that now I was rubbing it in about her breaking the jug. It was all so unfair! I suddenly wished I could click my fingers and find myself having breakfast with Dad, chatting about nothing much with a lovely big mug of tea and *no* half-brothers or sisters messing things up. I hoped he would ring today. It was odd that he hadn't phoned yesterday evening, but maybe the plane was delayed and he thought it too late to ring. It cheered me up to think that I'd be able to talk to him soon.

'What time's Ollie coming?' Toby piped up.

'Any time now,' said Nigel. Then he glanced at his watch and stood up quickly. 'It's later than I thought.'

'That's because of Lissie being naughty,' said Toby.

I could have killed him. 'I have *not* been naughty,' I muttered. 'It's just that nobody believes me.'

'Well, look at it from my point of view, Lissie,' said Mum, raising her voice. 'What do you expect me to think?'

*Did she really want to know?*

The doorbell rang.

'That'll be Ollie,' said Nigel.

*Lucky for you! Mum.*

# 7 ENTER OLLIE

I don't usually come across Ollie on my weekends at mum's, because he generally visits Nigel, his dad, on the weekends when I'm at home with *my* dad. I'd seen him a few times but we'd never really had any conversation, so I'd no idea what he was like.

He's got a ten-year-old brother called Rory, who's really funny. When he and Ollie were over once on the same Saturday as me, I remember Petronella following Rory around everywhere he went. In the end Rory turned to her and said, 'I'm just going to the toilet, Nellie. Want to come?' Petronella had gone bright red, stamped her foot and said, 'Don't call me Nellie! No one's allowed to call me Nellie.' And Rory had just laughed.

Right now Rory was at a sleepover at a friend's house so Ollie had come on his own. Toby held his hand and led him into the kitchen proudly while I was loading the dishwasher.

'That's Lissie,' Toby informed Ollie, pointing at me.

'I know,' said Ollie, casting his eyes to the ceiling then smiling at me.

'Hi,' I said, wondering what else to say.

'Sit down, Oliver,' said Nigel. 'Is the kettle on, Lissie?'

'I'll put it on. Who wants what?'

'Not *more* sitting down,' said Toby. 'Let's go and play football in the garden, Ollie.'

Toby was trying to drag Ollie out of his chair.

'Leave Ollie alone, Tobes,' said Nigel. 'I want to talk to him. Go and play on your own for a bit.'

Toby, true to form, ignored his father and kept tugging away violently at Ollie's sleeve.

'I'll play later,' said Ollie. 'Get off!'

He shook Toby off roughly, which made me want to break into applause. Nigel didn't notice. He was too busy asking Ollie about the results of tests and homework marks. I felt quite sorry for him because Nigel sounded so different from when he talked to Petronella and Toby. Did this big interrogation happen every time his son visited? I hoped not, for his sake.

'Can I have a go on your computer, Dad?' asked Ollie eventually.

'Aw, you said you'd play football in the garden with me!' said Toby.

'No, *you* said that, Toby,' Ollie pointed out calmly.

At that point Petronella left the kitchen. I bet I knew where she was going. I went to the dining-room where the computer was. Sure enough, there she was, clicking away, eyes glued to the screen. Selfish little girl!

I went back to the kitchen. Toby, Nigel and Ollie were trying to decide whether to walk up to the football field and watch the match or play football out in the garden.

'D'*you* want to play?' Ollie asked me.

'Yeah, OK,' I answered, feeling quite pleased to have been asked.

'She's a girl,' said Toby.

'Spotted,' I said under my breath, which made Ollie snigger.

'Yeah, let's all play football,' said Ollie, heading for the back door.

I followed him, and Toby shot past us both

to get the football from the shed. He also got out two old rounders stumps and Ollie stuck them in the ground to show where the goal was. It was clear they'd played before.

'I'll just watch,' I said.

''S'OK,' said Ollie, 'I'll be goalie. You two take turns to try and score goals.' So we did, and it was good fun. At one point Ollie kicked the ball a bit too hard and it hit Toby's arm.

'Ouch!' screeched Toby, his eyes going straight to the kitchen window to see if Mum was watching. She was. He clutched his arm and looked as though he was about to burst into tears. *Here we go!* I thought.

'If you go crying to your mum, that'll be the end of this game,' said Ollie, keeping the ball in the air with his feet and his knees, which I thought was really impressive.

Toby immediately let go of his arm and carried on with the game as though nothing had happened. Mum appeared at the back door.

'Are you all right, Tobes?'

He nodded.

'Well just remember he's only five, you two,' said Mum.

Olllie didn't say anything. Then Petronella appeared behind Mum.

'Can I play?'

'Of course you can, darling,' said Mum.

'I thought you were playing on the computer, Petronella,' I couldn't resist saying.

She scowled at me. 'I've finished now.'

I saw Ollie roll his eyes. He obviously didn't have any more patience with Petronella than I did.

'I think I'll have a go on the computer now it's free,' said Ollie. 'Coming, Lissie?'

'Yeah, OK.'

I smiled at him and he grinned back. It was

like the signing of a pact. I followed him into the house and the last thing I saw before shutting the back door was two wide-eyed, open-mouthed faces.

'Serves 'em right,' said Ollie softly as we went through to the dining-room. Mum and Nigel had seen us both go through, and they looked about as shocked as their children.

Yesss! An ally at last!

# 8 THE MATCH

Ollie and I were left in peace for about ten minutes, but during that time we did a lot of whispering about my mum and his dad. I wished I'd known sooner that my stepbrother was so great. I mean, he was just like an ordinary boy, but the good thing was that he understood how I felt about Petronella and Toby.

'Toby's not too bad though, is he?' said Ollie.

'Not half as bad as Petronella,' I agreed. 'He's used to getting his own way, that's all.'

'You're right there. I reckon his biggest problem is his parents – my dad and your mum. As far as *Pepsi* and *Tobes* are concerned they're far too much of a soft touch. I wish Dad was as easy-going with me as he is with those two, I can tell you.'

Ollie had said *Pepsi* and *Tobes* with a posh accent, making them sound more precious than ever.

'I must admit I was really surprised to hear Nigel quizzing you about all your school marks and everything,' I said.

'He's like that every time I come. It's as though he has one rule for those two and another one for me.' I nodded, knowing exactly what he meant. Ollie had been staring at the computer screen, but he suddenly gave me a sideways look through his floppy fringe. 'Is your mum like that with you?'

I nodded and we were both quiet for a

few seconds. 'It's just that . . .'

'Yeah?' he encouraged me.

'Well, now I'm here for a whole fortnight, it's much worse than usual. She's acting like I'm the devil's daughter. And it's all because of Petronella.'

'Why? What's she done?'

He was looking at me so sympathetically that I found myself spilling everything out to him. I told him about Toby trapping his finger, about the gravy boat and the whole dinner party nightmare, and when I explained about the torn coat, he gave a low whistle as though he couldn't believe it.

'But it's the little things too,' I gabbled on. 'It's really hard to explain and you'll probably think I'm stupid, but it's like she's trying to score points over me. I mean, I know she's only eight, but she's so . . . kind of cunning.'

I could feel my cheeks going pink and my

heart was beating faster than usual. I didn't want Ollie to think I was being too hard on Petronella.

'What kind of little things?' he asked me, frowning.

'Oh, you don't want to know!'

'Yes, I do – honestly.'

I focused on the far wall, and my mind seemed to fill up with Petronella's words:

*Tomorrow we'll go back to eating things that Toby and me like.*

*I'm quiet too, Mummy. Look at me.*

*By the time I'm Lissie's age my memory'll probably be better than hers, won't it?*

*I'll get them. You don't know where they are.*

*Lissie's daddy's gone away on holiday with his girlfriend.*

There were so many examples and by the time I'd finished there was a big lump in my throat. I had to swallow and look down so

Ollie wouldn't see what a baby I was.

'Wow, she *has* got a problem,' he said quietly. 'It sounds like she's really jealous of you.'

I felt tears come into my eyes when Ollie said that. It was just so brilliant to talk to someone who understood.

'But why is she jealous? What have I done?'

'It's not what you've done, it's who you are. She doesn't like sharing her mother with you.'

'But she's been doing that all her life and it's never been as bad as this.'

'Maybe she doesn't mind about the odd Saturday, but a whole fortnight seems a bit too permanent for her. And because she doesn't want you around, she does everything she can to draw attention to herself – like lying about on cushions and not going to bed.'

I was quiet while I thought about what Ollie

had just said, and tried to see things from Petronella's point of view.

'When do you go?' Ollie asked me a moment later.

'I only came yesterday. My life won't be worth living if she keeps up this horrible treatment for the whole fortnight.'

'Why don't you try talking to her. You know – see if you can make her your friend.'

We didn't have time to say any more after that because Mum came in and said that Pepsi and Tobes wanted to go and watch the local football match and then have a pub lunch.

As soon as she'd gone out, Ollie mimicked her voice and said, 'Oh well, if that's what Pepsi and Tobes want, we'd better all jump to it!'

I couldn't help laughing.

There were loads of parents watching the

football because it was the juniors playing. Mum spotted a friend of hers and went over to chat. The rest of us followed and stood close by to watch the match. Nigel was totally into it, calling out things to encourage the home team. Petronella skipped along the touch-line, singing a pop song. Toby stayed glued to Ollie's side. It was clear he adored him. He copied Ollie every time he clapped or called out 'Yes!' or punched the air. It was so funny to watch.

After a while, Petronella started tapping Mum's arm and whining that she wanted to go over to the adventure playground on the other side of the field. Mum was involved with her conversation with her friend.

'Off you go then, darling . . .' she said distractedly.

But Petronella started tugging on Mum's hand so Mum had to tug in the opposite direction to stop herself from falling over.

'I want you to come with me,' whined Petronella.

'Just wait till half time, Pepsi, and then Mummy will take you.'

'It's all right, I don't mind taking her,' I said, feeling sorry for Mum.

'No! Mummy!' said the adorable child, stamping her foot. 'I don't want Lissie. I want *you*!'

So what did Mum do? She gave in. Just like that! She shot her friend a rather embarrassed smile then allowed herself to be dragged away. As she went, I didn't miss the triumphant look that Petronella tossed in my direction.

'See what I mean?' I whispered to Ollie.

'You're not kidding,' he agreed. 'That girl's a real pain. But your mum's just making her worse.'

Nigel, of course, was oblivious to all that

was going on. He was keener on pointing out the players' tactics to Ollie.

'Did you see that, Ollie? That's the kind of thing you should be trying out when you're in matches at school. You see how he used his left foot? It's very important to get plenty of practice with your weaker foot. I hope the teacher tells you that.'

Ollie mumbled something.

'What? Doesn't the sports teacher teach you these things, Oliver?'

'Yeah . . . It's just that I prefer to play in goal, Dad.'

'No, you don't want to be in goal. You want to play up front. That's where the action is. You want to be a striker.'

Ollie turned to me and shrugged his shoulders as if to say, *What's the point? He's not even listening to me.*

This was a side of Nigel I'd never come

across. Not only did he want Ollie to do brilliantly well at school, he also wanted him to be a fantastic footballer – but not in goal. The moment the match was finished Nigel went back to the car and got the football.

'Come on, Ollie, let's give you a bit of practice,' he said.

Toby and Petronella were both playing in the adventure playground with Mum, which left me at a bit of a loose end. I quite liked football.

'Can I join in?' I asked, jogging alongside Ollie.

Our teacher at school always encouraged girls to play, so I knew the rules and I wasn't too bad at it.

'Yeah, see if you can get a goal,' said Ollie, running off to be keeper.

I dribbled the ball along, knowing that Nigel was watching me, but not sure what kind of expression he was wearing because my eyes were on the ball.

'Bet you won't get it past me,' said Ollie, leaning forward ready for a tricky save.

I waited till the last minute then I kicked a low one to the right of the goal. Ollie hurled himself sideways and reached out for the ball. His hand shot out and he managed to knock the ball out of the way. He landed on the ground, rolled over and jumped up.

'What a save!' he cried, punching the air.

We both looked over at Nigel.

'Well done, Ollie. Very good save, I agree. But let's try some proper play now. Here, throw the ball over. That's it. Now try and tackle me, OK?'

Ollie and I set off at the same time in pursuit of Nigel. I was much nearer so I got there first and tried to get the ball off him.

'Let Ollie have a go, eh, Lissie? I just want

to give him a bit of serious practise, then we can have a kick around for fun later.'

I stopped in my tracks, feeling suddenly knee-high to a grasshopper. Nigel was treating me like a little girl who was getting in the way of the big boys' game. Then, to add insult to injury, who should come charging back from the adventure playground but Little Miss Selfish!

'Kick it to me, Daddy,' she said, rushing up to Nigel and Ollie, who were both doing some clever footwork. She started jumping up and down, clapping and shouting, 'Come on, Daddy. Over here!'

Nigel laughed and said, 'You're far too young for this, Pepsi!'

'No I'm not, I'm just the right age!' shouted Petronella, grinning her head off and jumping even more wildly.

'Oh, all right, *you* win!' said Nigel, giving

in to his little angel. Big surprise!

I walked away from the happy little game that I hadn't been allowed to join but Petronella *had*, feeling like the biggest reject on the face of the earth. I'd only gone two paces when I came across Mum returning from the adventure playground.

'What's that miserable face all about?' she asked me.

'Doesn't matter,' I muttered, turning away.

'Yes it does,' Mum persisted, looking none too pleased. 'What is it, Lissie?'

'Well if you want to know, I'm just getting a bit sick of the two different sets of rules in this family,' I told her coldly.

Mum's hackles rose. 'And what exactly is that supposed to mean?'

'That Petronella always gets her own way. That's what.'

I couldn't help it, I was really mad. The

others were laughing and shouting as they kicked the ball about and it made me feel even more of an outcast.

'*I'll* kick it to you, Toby,' said Petronella in her sickly sweet voice, laid on specially for Mum's benefit, I presumed.

Mum took one look at the fun they were having and I knew exactly what she must have been thinking – that I was behaving like a silly little girl, being jealous of an eight-year-old. My head felt as though it was bursting with frustration. Mum just didn't understand how I felt, and I knew it was hopeless to try and explain. She could only see things from Petronella's point of view, and her next words proved it.

'Look, Lissie, I'm sorry, but Nigel and I aren't going to change the way we are, just because you're here for longer this time. I don't know why you consider yourself hard done by. Just go and join in with the others. No one's stopping you, are they?'

I couldn't believe my ears. I gave her my most withering, disgusted look and said, 'You just don't get it, do you, Mum?'

Then I stomped off.

# 9 MAKING A RESOLUTION

The rest of that Sunday was a mixture of good and bad. Mum was definitely much cooler towards me, and Nigel was different too. Quieter. I bet Mum had had a word with him about my 'attitude'. Petronella sensed that I wasn't exactly in her parents' best books, and played on it like mad. She acted all syrupy sweet and goodie two shoes, as though she was going for the best daughter of the year award. And every time she earned her parents' praise, her big eyes turned on me, pouring her smugness all over me. It was truly sick-making.

To make matters worse, she was subtly drawing Toby into her secret campaign against the presence of older half-sisters. He didn't really get what was going on but he enjoyed all the attention Petronella was giving him, so he played along.

'Toby and me have eaten all our dinner up, so we're allowed pudding, aren't we?' Petronella said at lunchtime in the pub.

Mum and Nigel had already told us all that we were just having a main course and no pudding because Mum was cooking a meal at six o'clock. I looked at her to see what she was going to say to Petronella. Our eyes met and she must have seen the challenge I was throwing at her. *Right, Mum, let's see if you give in or not.*

'We're not having puddings, Petronella,' said Mum firmly.

*What a surprise! Can she keep it up?*

'But I specially ate up all my first course because that's always the rule.'

'But this time your mum did say no puddings, Petronella,' Ollie pointed out. I was glad that someone else had said it, so that Mum realised I wasn't the only one to think that Petronella was spoilt.

'Well, I suppose it *is* a special occasion . . .' said Nigel. 'I mean, it's not often we have all six of us together, is it?'

'But we're not all together because Rory's not here,' Toby pointed out.

'Well, nearly all together.'

'I'll have treacle tart,' Petronella informed Nigel. 'What do you want, Toby?' she asked her little brother. She pointed to the blackboard on the wall. 'Look, you can have treacle tart or ginger sponge or Black Forest gat . . . gat . . .'

'Gateau, darling,' said Mum.

And so in the end we all had puddings. Mum deliberately avoided my gaze for the rest of the meal.

'Did you really mean it about trying to make Petronella my friend?' I asked Ollie, when we finally got a chance to talk on our own later.

'Yeah. I know it must seem impossible right now, but I've been thinking about it, and it seems like you've got two choices – either you don't do anything, which'll make the rest of the fortnight here seem like a prison sentence, or you try and get Little Miss Moanyguts on your side.'

'I can't see that working,' I told him, wrinkling my nose.

'I know it's a terrible thought,' said Ollie, 'but I reckon it'll be worth it. Give me a ring during the week and let me know how you're getting on.'

After Ollie had gone, I decided to practise my cello. The next day I had to play it for the first heat of the inter-house music competition. Our school has got a strong music department with lots of good musicians. All the students are divided into four houses called Regis, Crossland, Warburton and Bushstead, named after nearby forests. I'm in Crossland.

The highest scorers in the first heat go through to the second one, then only one person from each house goes through to the final. All the parents are invited to the final and it's on Wednesday evening at school. I'm crossing my fingers that I'll get into it even though I don't think I stand any chance because, like I said to Dad, it's usually only sixth-formers or Year Elevens who make it.

I was about to go and practise in my room (or Petronella's room – how could I forget?) when the phone rang. Nigel answered it.

'It's your dad, Lissie.'

I took the phone excitedly and went into the living-room to talk in peace.

'Hi, Dad. Are you having a great time? Where are you phoning from?'

He laughed. 'Yes to the first question. We're having a brilliant time. And I'm phoning from the hotel bedroom.'

'The line is so clear, it sounds like you're just next door.'

It was lovely to hear Dad's voice. I'd been quite sad when I'd gone to bed the previous evening and remembered that Dad had assured me he'd phone when they got there, and yet he hadn't.

'What have you been doing, Liss?'

Half of me felt like pouring my heart out to him but the other half didn't want to worry him. I put on my bright voice and told him the good bits of the day.

'It's been good because Ollie was here visiting his dad and we get along really well.'

'Great! And will he be around next weekend too?'

'No, it's not his weekend.'

'Oh well . . . And how are the other two behaving themselves?'

At that very moment – wouldn't you just know it? – in walked Petronella. She sat down at the table with a book that she'd brought in, and started reading – or should I say eavesdropping? Thank goodness it was a portable phone. I went upstairs into Mum and Nigel's room.

'Is it really hot out there, Dad?'

'Certainly is! The temperature's in the eighties during the day. First thing we did when we got here was to plunge into the pool.'

'Then what did you do?'

'Er . . . let me see . . . we had something to eat, then phoned you.'

'You phoned me yesterday?'

'Yes, didn't you get the message?'

'No. What time did you ring?'

'It must have been about ten o'clock. So it would have been nine o'clock for you.'

I thought back to the previous evening. The phone had rung when I'd been getting Toby back to bed. No one had said a word to me, so I'd just assumed it was for Mum or Nigel.

'Who answered the phone, Dad?'

'Petronella.'

That did it! There was no way I was going to try and befriend that girl now. I bet she deliberately didn't tell me. But of course, I'd never be able to prove it, because she'd swear blind she'd just forgotten. And if I dared to criticise her or get cross, Mum would say I was being unreasonable. I really was in a no-win situation.

'Write down this number, Liss, then if ever

you want to contact me, you can.'

When I'd said 'bye to Dad I went downstairs. Petronella came rushing out of the living-room. She must have been listening out for my footsteps.

'Sorry, Lissie, I just remembered that I forgot about your daddy ringing. You see, you were with Toby and I didn't want to disturb you, and then I forgot and never ever thought about it until right now.'

I looked at her carefully. Did I believe her? I wasn't sure. She was giving me a very innocent look.

'It's OK. It doesn't matter,' I said, sighing to myself, because I couldn't be bothered to be angry. I was fed up with being cross all the time. And funnily enough I felt better for having let Petronella off the hook. She was looking at me in quite a different way from usual, which made me think back to what Ollie had said. Maybe he was right. Perhaps this would be a good moment to try and make a truce.

'I'm going to do some cello practice, Petronella. Do you want to come and listen for a little while? I could show you how to play a few notes if you want.'

She was looking at me as though I'd turned into a magic fairy and was offering her three wishes, which made me feel a bit guilty. Maybe I'd been too hard on her before. I made a resolution then and there to be much more patient and see if the two of us could be friends.

# 10 THE MOSQUITO

I'd spent the last fifteen minutes telling Petronella the name of every part of my cello, showing her how to tune it with the knobs at the top, then how to draw the bow across the string, how to pluck a string, how to play a high note and a low note. I'd also taught her how to put the T under the chair to anchor the cello by sticking the spike in one of the holes of the T. She was fascinated by everything I told her, which made it a pleasure to have her around.

*We really are getting on well* I thought with surprise, as I began to play my piece. I'd told Petronella that the lesson was over and that now I was practising. I explained to her that when I practised I had to concentrate very hard on what I was doing and that the tiniest sound distracted me. I'd added that she could stay if she wanted, but that she might get a bit bored because I didn't want her to talk. She'd said that was fine and promised she wouldn't talk. She'd just sit on the bed and listen.

I thought it was too good to last. She interrupted me when I was on bar 27.

'Why do you like your cello so much?'

I stopped playing.

'I like it because it's my very own instrument and no one else plays it except me,' I said, trying to keep the impatience out of my voice. 'I must practise now, Petronella, so if you stay here you have to be quiet. OK?'

She nodded and made a big thing of lifting her bottom lip right up high over the top one, to show me how impossible it would be for any words to escape the tightly closed mouth. I thought it was quite sweet, and then felt surprised again. A few hours before I'd never have imagined I could possibly find my half-sister sweet. I looked at my music, got focused and started the piece again.

About a minute into the piece I heard a high-pitched sound which I thought was a mosquito. I frowned and tried to push the noise out of my mind, but it wouldn't go away. It was getting louder in fact, and driving me mad. I was torn between stopping and finding the stupid insect, and just trying to ignore it. I focused all my attention on the music but it was impossible to concentrate because the mosquito had suddenly turned into the most talented insect I'd ever come across, humming a whole bunch of notes. The mosquito had to be Petronella. My patience was really being put to the test here.

'Look, Petronella, if you can't keep quiet can you just go, please? I can't practise with you humming like that.'

'I wasn't humming. I never made a sound, honestly. I've just been sitting here as quiet as a little mouse. Honest.'

I narrowed my eyes and stared at her. 'So what was that humming noise then? You must have heard it if *I* did.' She shrugged. I tried to put on a kinder, less accusing voice. 'Are you certain it wasn't you, Petronella?'

'Positive.'

'So how come the noise has stopped now?'

'I don't know. I didn't even hear a noise. Perhaps the noise is coming from inside your head.'

She looked so innocent that I began to get

worried. Perhaps the noise *was* coming from inside my head. Maybe there was something wrong with my ears. Suddenly it seemed terribly important to pinpoint the noise.

'Right, let's try again, shall we? I'll play the cello. You keep quiet. Got it?'

This time I wasn't concentrating on the music at all. My antennae were twitching for all they were worth, trying to pick up sounds which definitely weren't coming from inside my head. I played through the whole piece without hearing a single thing. But it couldn't be called practising, what I was doing, because I wasn't thinking about my music at all.

'It's no good, Petronella, you'll have to go. I'm sorry, but you're distracting me.'

'I'm not even doing anything. It's not fair.'

'Aren't you bored?'

'No, I like the cello. I want to learn it. I'm going to ask Mummy if I can learn, then I can practise on your cello, can't I?'

'My cello's far too big for you. If you learnt the cello you'd have to get a half-sized one, or even a quarter-size to start with.'

'That's a stupid idea. They must be for babies. Look, I can play yours easily.'

And with that she grabbed the bow out of my hand and started grinding it up and down the string as though she was sawing a huge tree trunk.

'Stop it, Petronella. You'll ruin it!' I screeched.

But she didn't stop. She carried on sawing away and humming loudly at the same time. I recognised the humming. The mosquito mystery was solved, and I was at the end of my tether. The trouble was, I was stuck in my chair with the cello firmly wedged between Petronella and me. If I tried to get up I'd be pushing the cello towards her which would make the damage she was doing even worse.

There was only one thing for it. I raised my right leg, turned my foot inwards and kicked her on the bottom. She let out the most ear-piercing scream and looked daggers at me. I'd hardly touched her, because it was too difficult from that angle, but she was acting like I'd sent her flying across the room. Only a second later she crumpled into tears and stood there looking like the poor wronged little sister. And that was when Mum appeared. Perfect timing as ever.

'I . . . didn't . . . know . . . I wasn't allowed . . . to . . . use . . . the . . . bow, Mummy,' Petronella sobbed dramatically, rubbing her bottom.

'What did you do to her?' Mum asked me in a horribly low voice.

'I hardly touched her.'

'I see. And is that why she's sobbing her heart out?'

'She kicked me on the bottom, Mummy.'

Mum took Petronella's hand and went and cuddled her on the bed. 'Poor baby,' she whispered into Petronella's curly hair.

'*Poor baby* was actually ruining my practice, Mum. She kept interrupting when I'd told her not to.'

'I only interrupted once to ask Lissie why she loved her cello so much. I was interested, that's all.'

Mum didn't say anything, but the look she gave me said, *And is that so very unreasonable?*

'She started humming – pretending to be a mosquito.'

A new set of tears sprang into Petronella's eyes and started running down her face. She really should take up acting. Casting directors must be crying out for little kids who could turn on the waterworks at the drop of a hat like she could.

'But I *didn't* hum, Mummy. Lissie must have imagined the humming. It wasn't me, honest.'

One look at Mum's face and I knew there was no point in defending myself any further. She'd made up her mind that Petronella was telling the truth and that I was turning into a monster — a horrible half-sister monster.

'Come on, darling,' she said to Petronella. 'Let's go and help Daddy with the crossword, and leave Lissie to finish her practice.'

Petronella scrambled down from Mum's lap dutifully and clutched her hand to walk past me, as though she might be in danger of another walloping if she risked it alone.

'I'll speak to you later,' Mum added icily. Then she shut the door behind her.

I hung my head over my cello and felt my own tears gathering behind my eyes. Only mine were genuine. I couldn't bear to live in this household for another thirteen days, especially now it felt like Mum didn't really want me there!

Right, Miss Petronella Banks – I've tried being kind and friendly and that doesn't work. Now for something completely different.

# 11 VANDALISM

On Monday morning before registration the usual group of us sat round talking about the weekend. As always I could feel myself tensing up because it was about to be my turn. They'd all think I'd been at Dad's this weekend because they knew I was at Mum's last weekend. Loads of times in the past week I'd thought about telling them that I was going to be at Mum's for a whole fortnight, because it was going to be impossible to keep it a secret for all that time. But every time I'd been about to open my mouth I'd chickened out.

If I'd had a proper best friend it would have been so much easier, but it was like Leanne and Donna were best friends and so were Gemma and Jo. They were really nice to me and drew me into their circle, but I still felt like an outsider. If only one of them had divorced parents that would have made it easier.

Right now, I really wished I *had* told them. The trouble was, they were going to feel doubly sorry for me because not only had I had another weekend at Mum's, I'd also got the rest of the fortnight to go! I'd just have to pretend I was having a great time and that everything was fine. If only I could be like Leanne and tell the truth but laugh about it. I'd still be pretending, only it would be a different sort of pretending. I'd be admitting that I was having an awful time, but pretending I didn't care. Only really I did care. I cared terribly.

We were sitting on the tables, taking turns to speak. Any minute now it would be my turn. My palms felt sweaty and my heart was beating much more loudly than usual.

'You were at your dad's this weekend, weren't you, Lissie?' said Donna, smiling.

'No, I was at my mum's actually.'

They were all looking at me.

'Oh, poor you,' said Jo. 'Two weekends on the trot!'

*Go on, Lissie, say it. Tell the truth.*

I took a deep breath.

'It wouldn't be too bad if it was just two weekends on the trot, but it's a whole fortnight, worse luck, because Dad's away.'

'You don't really . . . like it at your mum's, do you?' said Gemma hesitantly.

'Normally I don't like it much, but this weekend was the pits, thanks to my nauseating little half-sister.'

There! I'd said it. The world hadn't collapsed around me, but all four of my friends were staring at me wide-eyed. Leanne leaned forwards.

'Petronella, isn't it?'

I nodded.

'What's wrong with her?' asked Donna.

I sighed. 'Her parents, I suppose.'

'But hang on a sec! You and she have got the same mum, haven't you?' said Leanne.

'Yeah, only sometimes it doesn't feel like it.'

Nobody said anything, but they were all looking at me so sympathetically that I carried on, and before I knew it I'd told them all about the dinner party, the rip in the coat, the gravy boat, the phone call, the football, Ollie, the pub lunch and the cello.'

'Blimey, Lissie! She sounds a right little monster,' said Leanne. 'I don't think I'd have been that patient with her.'

'I don't think I'd have been as patient with my *mum*,' added Donna.

'And Toby sounds a bit of a pain as well,' commented Jo.

'But at least you had Ollie,' said Gemma.

'Yeah, that's true,' I said. 'Only I won't see him again this fortnight because he only comes every other weekend.'

'Couldn't you phone him up and beg?' laughed Leanne. '*I* would. I'd be on my bended knees, pleading down the phone.'

I couldn't help laughing, especially when Jo pointed out that there wouldn't be much point in getting down on bended knees, because he wouldn't be able to see from the other end of the phone. Then we got on to the subject of video phones and cameras in computers, so my problem was forgotten.

Inside, I was dancing with happiness though, because I suddenly felt like one of the gang, not a spectator. And the dancing grew wild when the bell went and everyone sat in their places, because Leanne whispered, 'Don't worry, Liss, we'll think of something. Talk to you at break, OK?'

It was lovely to know that they cared about me. I only wished I'd told them all about everything sooner.

At break time we all met up in the science lab because Jo had to finish off an experiment and write up the conclusion. The lab assistant is really nice and always lets people work in there at break times.

'Jo and me have had a great idea,' Leanne announced, watching the liquid in Jo's test tube, which was slowly turning dark yellow. 'We reckon you ought to invite us all round to your mum's place after school one day, then we can suss out Petronella for ourselves.'

I felt really happy, but there was one thing . . .

'It's quite a long bus ride,' I pointed out.

'That doesn't matter,' said Jo. 'And don't worry, we won't let Petronella get away with anything. She'll pretty soon realise that she's very lucky to have such a nice half-sister as you.'

'Yeah, and if your mum's too soft on her, we'll all make it clear we don't approve, by raising our eyebrows at each other, like this,' added Leanne, arching her eyebrows until her forehead wrinkled and her eyes nearly popped out of her head. The rest of us couldn't help laughing. Even the lab assistant was smiling to herself. Good old Leanne! She always made people happy.

It all sounded great. None of us had got any

after-school activities the next day, so the plan was that I'd ask Mum if they could come home on the bus with me and meanwhile they'd ask their parents if it was OK to be picked up from Mum's at about seven-thirty. If we had homework to do, we could all do it together.

There was only one thing I was worrying about now . . .

'I'm feeling really nervous about playing in the first heat of the music competition,' I admitted to Leanne and the others.

'You'll sail through,' Leanne said, giving me an unexpected hug.

'Yeah, Mr Crane will be as gobsmacked as we were when he hears you play on your own,' Jo added.

I felt so happy that they sounded as though they genuinely thought I was good. They'd insisted I play them a piece when they'd come to meet me after orchestra practice the other week. When I'd finished they'd praised me like mad. But hearing them compliment me now gave me an even better feeling. I didn't want to admit it, but I was fairly sure I'd get through the first heat. But the second one, the next day . . . That was another matter.

After lunch time I took my cello out of the instrument room and went along to the music room. Mr Crane had read out everybody's first-heat audition time in assembly and mine was one forty-five – the last one before afternoon school.

'Right, Melissa,' said Mr Crane, opening the door to let the last candidate out and me in. He was looking at his watch and I could tell he was in a hurry. Maybe he hadn't had any lunch and wanted to get to the canteen before it closed. My audition piece was very short because my cello teacher had told me that it was always best to do very short audition pieces so the person judging didn't have the chance to get bored.

I began to take my cello out of its case as fast as I could, but an icy feeling was going down my spine, because I could hear a rattling noise, and that meant something was wrong.

It felt as though all the blood had left my face when I saw what had happened. Instead of four strings tightly stretched as usual over the bridge, I was met with four dangling strings and no sign of the bridge at all. I looked inside the cello and saw that the bridge was in there.

I felt as though someone had punched me in the gut. This was deliberate vandalism. The kind of damage I was looking at simply couldn't happen on its own. The chances were that the sound post from inside the cello had been dislodged too and that would mean I'd have to take it to be repaired. But that would take days. My throat hurt, my head swam and

I sat there staring in disbelief and trying not to let the tears in my eyes drop on to my broken cello.

'Right, Melissa. All set?' asked Mr Crane, looking up. 'What the . . .? How ever did this happen?' He was shaking his head in bewilderment. He came over to peer at the cello. 'Do you know anything about it?' I shook my head and swallowed hard, trying not to cry. 'Did you leave the cello in the safe room?' I nodded again. I'd never dream of bringing my cello to school and not putting it in the safe room. You could only open the door by tapping in a code. Mr Crane looked at his watch again. 'So you're absolutely certain that when you came to school this morning your cello was all in one piece, Melissa?'

I thought back through the morning. The truth was that I couldn't be sure. I hadn't looked at it since I'd finished practising the previous evening. It had certainly been all right when I'd put it back in its case, but . . .

No! Surely Petronella wouldn't sink so low as to wreck my most precious possession. On the other hand, why should anyone at school do such a thing? I didn't have any enemies as far as I knew. It was a mystery. A horrible one.

'Look, I'll try to get to the bottom of this, Melissa,' said Mr Crane, going for the kindliest tone he could for a man in a big hurry. 'Borrow this school cello for now. It's a bit scratchy, but it'll have to do.'

He handed me a very battered-looking half-sized cello.

'I'm used to a full-sized, Mr Crane,' I whispered, feeling really wretched.

'I'm afraid beggars can't be choosers, Melissa. What's the name of your piece?'

'*The Swan.*'

'Right, off you go.'

The cello felt far too little and the strings were close together. I drew my bow across to play the first note and it bounced off the string because I was so shaky. I still felt like crying, partly because of what had happened to my cello, but mainly because of the thought of someone actually hating me enough to do that. The school cello was impossible to play. I tried to carry on with the piece but I just couldn't make the notes come out and after three false starts I gave up.

'Sorry, Sir. It doesn't feel right.'

'Bad luck, Melissa. I think we'd better call it a day, but rest assured, I'll make sure we get to the bottom of this problem. I'm not having people vandalising other people's property like this in my music department.'

'So didn't I . . . get through the heat?'

'Don't you worry about that. It tends to be sixth-formers in the finals, so you'll have plenty 'more opportunities in the coming years.'

'But . . . couldn't I get my cello mended and *then* show you? I'm much better on my own cello, honestly.'

'No time, I'm afraid, Melissa. We're on to the second heats tomorrow. You just concentrate on getting that cello mended and I'll concentrate on finding the culprit.'

He gave me a nice bright smile, and I left the room with a big lump in my throat, hating the world for being so unfair to me. I felt like running away from school without telling anyone. The only reason I didn't was because my name wasn't Leanne Goyder, it was Melissa Raines. And Melissa Raines didn't have the guts to do things like run away.

# 12 TACTICS

Going home on the bus that day, I stared out of the window deep in thought. Leanne and the others had been so sympathetic about my cello. Leanne even said she was going to kill the person who'd committed the crime when she found out who it was. It was great that she was being so friendly, but it didn't make up for what had happened. I thought back.

There definitely hadn't been an opportunity for Petronella to take it out of its case, unwind all four strings and put it back in the case before school. She'd never been out of my sight for more than a couple of minutes. She wouldn't have dared to risk it. So maybe it *was* someone at school. But it was a bit of a coincidence that no one had ever harmed my cello in any way whatsoever, and suddenly Petronella hates me and – surprise, surprise – my cello gets damaged!

I went over the previous evening carefully. When I'd finished my practice I'd gone downstairs to find the others all watching television together. Petronella was snuggled up to Mum on the settee and Toby was sitting on Nigel's knee in the big armchair. I'd sat in the other chair, feeling like an unwanted visitor. Petronella and Toby had had baths, but I thought Mum had been with them at that time so unless Petronella had got up in the middle of the night, I didn't see when she could have done it. I'm a very light sleeper though; I think I would have heard her dragging the cello out of its case.

When I got home I found Mum and Petronella in the kitchen. Toby was watching television in the other room.

'Hello, Lissie,' said Mum. But her voice was flat. It was obvious she wasn't exactly filled with joy at the sight of me. I tried to smile and make my voice bright and cheerful.

'Hi, Mum. Hi, Petronella.'

Petronella gave me a suspicious look, and this was my first clue. She hadn't expected me to be so cheerful. *I wonder why?* It looked as though I'd surprised Mum too with my cheery voice. She'd probably thought I was still going to be in a sulk over the mosquito episode.

'How did you get on in the first heat?' she asked me in a warmer voice.

'I couldn't do it, Mum,' I said, still smiling away as I opened the cello in full view of them both. I watched their faces closely. 'You see, someone has broken my cello.'

Mum gasped and her hands flew to her mouth at the sight of the damage. A second later, Petronella did exactly the same thing. What a giveaway! I stared at her coldly. When her eyes met mine she went red, then looked defiant and turned away. Mum caught my look. (It was impossible to miss.)

'Why are you looking like that, Lissie?'

'Oh Mum, isn't it obvious why?' I knew I was sounding exasperated.

'No, it isn't. What are you saying?'

'Mum, the cello is locked up at school, and it's never ever been touched before. Now, all of a sudden, Petronella hates me and my cello is broken. A chimpanzee could work it out. Why can't you?'

The moment the words were out of my mouth I knew I'd gone too far. I'll never forget the way Mum's face turned pale with two red spots high on her cheeks. Then, even though the rest of her was still and tense, her face started shaking. I think it was a mixture of anger and shock. When she spoke her voice was horribly quiet.

'I never thought I'd have to say this to you, Lissie, especially at your age, but go to your room.'

My eyes met Petronella's and I saw the triumph there. I wanted to throw up.

'How can I go to my room? I haven't got one,' I told Mum harshly. And then I walked out of the back door and down the road. Fifty metres later I turned the corner and started running towards the little lane that led to Galley Stream. I sat on the bridge staring at the water, my legs dangling. Even then I didn't cry. I felt strangely calm. It was as though I knew I had to conserve my energy to fight this battle and crying wouldn't help.

Twenty minutes later I was on a payphone in town.

'Hi, Ollie! it's Lissie.'

'Hi! How's it going?'

'Terrible.'

I told him the whole story as fast as I could.

'Wow!' he said at the end. 'It's like your mum's living in cloud cuckoo land.'

'I wish you could come over, Ollie.'

'There's no way – sorry. I've got two essays to hand in tomorrow and they're already late. Mum's going ape. I've asked if I can come this weekend though, and she said it was fine with her as long as Dad agrees.'

It was like a flicker of light in a nearly dead torch when Ollie said that.

'What do you think I should do, Ollie? Tell me quick – the money's about to run out.'

'What, you mean which method of torture

should you use? Chinese burns is a good one . . .'

'Don't muck about, Ollie . . .'

And then the money did run out. In one way Ollie had been no help at all, but in another way, he'd been great. I didn't feel so alone any more. I plotted my next move all the way home, and by the time I went in through the back door I reckoned all my anger and frustration was safely hidden, and I could convince Mum that I was very sorry. It was my only choice if I wanted my friends to come home with me the following day.

'Where ever have you been? I've been worried sick.' She looked it too. 'I was on the point of phoning the police, Lissie. We simply cannot carry on like this.'

'Sorry, Mum.'

I could tell she hadn't been expecting me to apologise just like that. I'd taken the wind out of her sails. She couldn't be cross with me now.

'Look, Lissie, sit down and tell me once and for all why you've got it in for Petronella.'

We were on our own in the kitchen. It took all my willpower not to scream at her that she'd got it totally wrong and that I didn't have it in for Petronella – Petronella had it in for me! And precious little Petronella was an evil little toad who was twisting her silly naïve parents right round her little finger.

'I don't want to argue with you, Mum, but if I say anything at all against Petronella I know it will make us argue.'

Mum opened her mouth to speak but then shut it again. I think I'd surprised her once more by not coming up with what she was expecting.

'You can't go around accusing people of doing things when you haven't got an ounce of proof, Lissie. Petronella is very upset that you think she's responsible for the damage to your cello. How ever could a little eight-year-old do all that? And *when,* for goodness' sake? Not to mention *why?*'

All the arguments in my head were screaming to be let out but I had to keep telling myself that my friends would never be allowed to come over if I made Mum mad again. I had to stay calm at all costs.

'Perhaps I was wrong, then. But why should anyone at school want to deliberately vandalise my cello?'

'Maybe someone was afraid that you might get through the heat instead of them.'

I frowned and tried to think if there could be any truth in what mum had just said. I really didn't think so. Surely no one was that competitive.

'Well, anyway, I didn't get through and now

I can't even practise. What should I do about getting my cello mended?'

I bit my lip because I was feeling upset again. Mum gave me a sympathetic look and said, 'I'll phone Mrs Martin and see what she suggests.'

'Sorry I ran off, Mum. I was just really upset.'

She looked right into my eyes for several seconds before speaking in a gentle, tired sort of voice.

'I know, love. It's OK. Just please don't ever do it again.'

She picked up the phone and tapped in the number, while I gave myself an imaginary pat on the back for keeping calm and getting back into her good books. I knew someone who wasn't going to be too pleased about that when she found out!

\* \* \*

That evening I tried to be as nice as possible to everyone, though Nigel continued to be fairly cool with me and Petronella ignored me, while being over-the-top goodie goodie for Mum and Nigel. Mum was acting reasonably normally, though she kept her eye on me, following me round quite a lot as though she was afraid I might make another bolt for it.

Mrs Martin had given Mum the name of a man who repairs cellos, and Mum was going to take the cello round to his workshop the next morning. Mrs Martin had already contacted him and he'd said that he thought he could get it mended by the end of the week. I was dreading having to get through a whole week with no Dad *and* no cello. I wouldn't even be able to play in the orchestra at the final of the music competition. There was hardly any point in going now – only that I was singing in the choir. I would have felt a bit more involved if I'd at least got through to the second heat.

Toby was being really sweet towards me and I couldn't work out why this sudden affectionate touch. When we were all watching television he got up and sat on my lap. The moment he was snuggled in, he turned and said, 'This is really good, isn't it, Lissie?' in his loudest voice right in my earhole.

'Yes, it's great, but don't shout, Toby,' I replied as gently as I could.

I pretended to be completely absorbed in the programme on television, but out of the corner of my eye I could see Petronella subtly patting the carpet beside her to try to get Toby to sit with her instead. She just couldn't help herself being selfish the whole time, and yet Mum and Nigel couldn't see it.

'What do you want, Petronella?' I asked her, which took her aback.

'Nothing,' she answered quickly.

Mum looked at us both, then she and Nigel exchanged glances. I bet they thought I was stirring things up or something. I just smiled at Mum, then asked her if it would be OK for me to have a few friends round the next day. I even offered to make the tea myself so it wouldn't be any extra trouble.

'No, that's fine, Lissie. I'd love to meet your school friends.'

I got the feeling she was quite pleased to find that I did actually have some friends!

# 13 CRANK

'This is my mum,' I introduced my friends as we walked into the kitchen after school the next day to find Mum ironing.

'Call me Sheila,' Mum said, smiling round.

'This is Leanne, Jo, Gemma and Donna,' I told Mum.

'I'll try to remember,' said Mum, 'but I'm pretty hopeless at names. Do you want to have some crisps or something to keep you going till tea time?'

At that point Petronella walked in.

Immediately all eyes were upon her. She smiled round, and said, 'Oh hello, you lot!' in such a surprised voice that Leanne and the others burst out laughing. 'Can I have some crisps, Mummy?'

'You've had yours already, haven't you, Pepsi!'

*Great!* I thought. *Here comes a perfect example of Mum letting Petronella get her own way.*

'Oh yes,' said Petronella, tapping her head and screwing up her eyes as though she was embarrassed to have forgotten. 'Silly me!'

I couldn't believe my ears. I expected Petronella to whine and moan at Mum and say it wasn't fair, and that she wanted another packet of crisps, and then Mum would give in. But the one time I really want her to behave badly, she turns on the charm.

'Why don't you put your bags in the utility room?' Mum said. 'You have to carry so much around these days, don't you, girls?'

'Well, some of us do,' Jo said, giving Leanne a pointed look.

'That's a dig at me, Sheila,' Leanne explained with a shrug. 'You see, most students carry books and things, but my bag's full of sweets and . . . personal stuff.'

'Leanne's got this little set of ornaments that she takes with her everywhere,' said Gemma.

'Well, I like them,' pouted Leanne. 'They're precious to me, they are.'

'Do you want to see Lissie's room?' Petronella asked everyone when we'd dumped our bags in the utility room. She then broke into a loud stage whisper: 'It's really my room, but I don't mind Lissie pretending it's hers just for today. I'll keep right out of your way, don't worry.' And with that she skipped out of the room, leaving all four of my friends totally enchanted with her.

I, on the other hand, felt like a big fraud.

The others were going to think I'd just been making it up about Petronella, she was acting so completely out of character. All I could hope was that it wouldn't last until seven-thirty when they all had to go.

But it *did* last. It was just as though someone had pressed Petronella's 'best behaviour' button and she couldn't put a foot wrong. She stayed out of our way most of the time, but when she *was* around, like at tea time, she behaved perfectly, offering to pass things, laughing at everyone's jokes and helping Toby cut up his pizza. In fact, she made me look stupid for ever having said anything bad about her. The moment tea was over I took the others up to our room.

'She's not usually like this. I can't believe the way she's acting,' I said, rolling my eyes at Leanne. I was expecting Leanne to sympathise and tell me it was really bad luck or something, but she just gave me a funny look as though I was out of my tiny mind.

'The moment you've gone she'll probably turn back into her usual *charming* self,' I added, feeling desperate. 'I wouldn't put it past her to be deliberately showing you how perfectly sweet she is, just to spite me.'

No one said anything, and I wished I hadn't made that last comment. I quickly put on a CD and we all chatted. But it wasn't as much fun as I'd hoped. It was as though I'd lost several points over the whole Petronella thing. So all in all it was quite a relief when seven-thirty came and Jo's mum turned up to take them all home.

'Thanks very much, Sheila,' they said.

''Bye, Pepsi. 'Bye, Tobes,' called Leanne.

And as the door shut behind them I sighed a big sigh and felt more lonely than ever.

'Can Lissie read to me?' asked Toby,

remembering to use his soft voice.

'Do you mind, Lissie, or have you got homework?' Mum asked me.

'No, I don't mind at all,' I said. And I really didn't. Toby seemed to be my one true friend at the moment.

He leaned his head against me as I read, and when he sucked his thumb noisily, it didn't get to me like it usually did.

'You like that story, don't you, Toby?' He nodded and kept his gaze on me for ages. 'What's the matter, Toby? Is something wrong?'

He opened his mouth to speak then shut it again and shook his head.

'Do you want another story?'

He nodded.

At morning break the following day I found myself on my own. The girls had been pretty off-hand before registration too. From the moment they left the house the previous evening I'd started getting scared that this might happen. It wasn't that they'd completely cut me off or anything like that. They were just much less chatty than usual, and the looks they gave me weren't particularly friendly. I went off in search of them, hoping that things might have miraculously improved a bit, and found them leaning against the wall, below the history rooms. Leanne had set her precious little ornaments out on the wall, but she didn't look too happy.

'She's lost Crank,' Jo explained.

I knew it wasn't very nice of me, but in a way I was pleased, because it took the focus off me. They were forgetting to be unfriendly in the light of this new crisis. And it *was* a crisis. Leanne had thirty-three ornaments at home and seven in her bag at all times, and she'd named every single one of them. Crank was her favourite.

'When did you last see it?' I asked.

'See *him*,' Leanne corrected me.

'She gets very touchy about that,' whispered Jo.

I could have danced with happiness because Jo, at least, was being normal with me.

'Well, I definitely had him at the end of school yesterday,' said Leanne.

'Did you take a register or something?' giggled Gemma.

'Stop taking the rise, you lot. You know how much I love my ornaments.'

'Sorry,' said Gemma, putting her arm round Leanne. 'Right, let's think hard about this. Are you double positive you saw it – sorry, *him* – at the end of school yesterday?'

'Yes, because when we were on the bus I ate that cereal bar, didn't I? And I saw that they 'were all there when I opened my school bag.'

'Well, maybe Crank dropped out then, without you realising it.'

'No, he definitely didn't. He was right at the bottom of the bag.'

'So when did you first notice he was missing?' I asked her.

'This morning in geography.' (Leanne wasn't in the same set as me for geography.) 'I got my geog books out, did a quick check and realised he was missing. I tell you, I didn't hear a word of what old Jonesy was on about, because I was trying to empty the entire contents of my bag into my lap without him seeing.'

'Do you think one of your brothers might have taken him for a joke?' asked Donna.

'No, they used to muck about like that when I started collecting ornaments, but they haven't time for things like that now. They're too busy with girlfriends. When I got home from Lissie's

I dumped my bag in my room and it stayed there all night. Then I picked it up this morning and came to school.'

'Which means . . .' said Jo thoughtfully, as all eyes turned on me, '. . . that it must have happened at Lissie's house.'

I felt my face turning pale. First I'm unpopular because of telling lies about my half-sister, now I'm an ornament thief. God had really got it in for me. Then something dawned on me. Maybe this would turn out to work in my favour. If the cunning little Petronella had taken Crank, this would be the very proof I needed to convince the others that she wasn't quite so cute as she made out.

'Our school bags were in the utility room the whole time at Lissie's house,' said Donna.

One by one they turned their eyes on me. It was obvious what they were all thinking, but no one wanted to say it, so I said it for them. I couldn't help a little note of triumph creeping into my voice.

'Exactly. Petronella. Now you know what she's like.'

'No, she can't have done . . .' said Leanne. 'She was so sweet. I just know she wouldn't do anything like that.'

'No, she's not, though. That's the whole point,' I tried to tell her. 'She was standing there, wasn't she, when Mum told us to dump our bags in the utility room? She heard what you said about having a bag full of ornaments and sweets.'

I watched as my friends' faces gradually took on puzzled expressions.

'I just can't imagine . . .' Donna began, but she faded out and no one else said anything more.

'I'll ask her about it tonight,' I said.

Leanne nodded.

# 14 THE TRUTH

I got off the bus and let myself into the house. Luckily, this was the day that Petronella did ballet, which meant that I'd got a good half hour to search her room for the missing Crank. I went about it systematically from one end to the other, looking in every bit of every drawer, even the drawers under her bed. I also looked among the bedclothes and under her pillow. I rummaged through all her clothes in the wardrobe and behind all her books on the bookshelves. Finally I had to admit defeat, and then I started to feel really horrible for invading her privacy. I wouldn't like it if someone did that to me.

They came in about ten minutes later and Toby practically threw himself at me.

'We've got your tello! We've got your tello!' he cried happily, clutching my hand.

It took me a few seconds to realise that he was talking about my cello. Toby's never been able to say the *ch* sound properly. An instant thrill of happiness came over me. 'Brilliant! Ready already? How come?' I asked Mum.

Petronella had walked straight past me and into the living-room. She'd switched the television on, turned the volume turned right up, and left the doors open.

'Turn that down, Pepsi!' Mum called through to her, but there was no change. 'She's excited because the ballet teacher asked her to do one of the exercises on her own, to show the others,' Mum explained, though what that had got to do with coming home and watching the telly on top volume, I had no idea.

'How come the cello's ready so soon?' I tried again, following Mum back out to the car to get it.

'I think the man is a good friend of Mrs Martin's and she must have told him you needed it urgently.'

I bit my lip. Mrs Martin didn't know that I hadn't even got through the first heat. All she knew was that it was the final tonight and she'd probably been hoping I'd be playing. By now, she must have realised I hadn't got through because I would have phoned her with the great news otherwise. I felt guilty for not phoning, but the truth was I was quite embarrassed. I'd tell her the next day in my lesson. Meanwhile, I could play my cello with the orchestra after all, so at least I wouldn't just be singing in the choir and doing nothing else but sitting in the audience for the rest of the big event. Now I was even happier.

Mum went into the living-room and turned the television down. I looked down at Toby, who was still clutching my hand tightly.

'I'm going to practise my cello, Toby,' I told him.

He let go of my hand so I could carry the cello, but he followed me upstairs and said I could practise in his room if I wanted. I took him up on that, and he sat on his bean bag in the corner as quiet as a little mouse for twenty-five minutes.

There were three pieces that I was practising and the last one reminded me of tropical seas, blue sky and sunshine. As soon as I started to play it I thought about Dad, and then I had a really big urge to phone him. I asked Mum if it would be all right, and she said it would be fine, so I got the phone from Mum and Nigel's room and came back to Toby's room. Toby had gone downstairs.

There was no reply. As I bent down to pick up my bow, something caught my eye. Poking out from under Toby's bed was a little green arm. My heart missed a beat and I stood rooted to the spot, not wanting to see what I was seeing. Finally I lunged forwards and picked up the green thing before I could change my mind. It was Crank.

My hand holding the ornament dropped to my side and all the happiness I'd just been feeling seemed to seep out of my body. I had never ever imagined that Toby might have taken Crank. I took a deep breath and went downstairs.

'That was good timing,' said Mum, as I went into the kitchen to find Petronella and Toby sitting at the table. 'You've just got time for a bite to eat. Suzanne will be here in about ten minutes.'

Suzanne was the mother of a girl in Year Seven, called Claire, who was singing in the choir in the finalists' concert. They only lived a couple of minutes away from Mum so she'd said it was no problem taking me to the concert as she was going anyway. Mum would have come herself if I'd been one of the finalists.

I sat down, Crank in my pocket, and ate the pancakes that Mum had made. As I ate I tried to think what to do. Maybe it would be easier just to give Crank back to Leanne and say no more about it, but the girls would want to know where I'd found it.

'How was your dad?' asked Mum.

'There was no reply.'

'Oh well, never mind. Perhaps you'll get hold of him after the concert.'

'So you couldn't tell your daddy that the

tello is all mended now,' said Toby.

I looked at his little anxious face. He really seemed to genuinely care about my cello and my happiness.

'Did you have a good practice?' asked Mum.

'Fine, thanks . . . But it was funny, because when I'd rung off from trying to get Dad, I bent down to pick up my bow and saw this tucked under Toby's bed.'

I held out my hand and slowly let my fingers uncurl. All three of them leant forwards to see the little green ornament lying in the palm of my hand. Petronella's eyes widened. It was clear she recognised it. So did Toby. His bottom lip trembled. Mum looked at them both, then back at me. The expression on her face was both worried and suspicious.

'What's this about?' she asked me softly.

'Leanne lost this. It's one of the little ornaments that she carries around with her.'

There was a silence, apart from Petronella's nonchalant munching on her French fries. For once Mum was stuck for words. She turned to Toby and spoke in a low voice.

'Did you take this out of Leanne's bag, Toby?'

Toby looked at Petronella, and so did I. Her eyes were boring into his little face. I couldn't work out what she was trying to tell him, but it was certainly something very urgent.

'Answer me, Toby,' said Mum sharply. And that did it.

Toby burst into tears.

'Petronella took it! She said I had to keep it in my room. She said I mustn't tell because . . . if I did . . .'

His crying grew stormier.

'What would happen if you did, Toby?' asked Mum extremely sharply.

'If I did . . . she'd tell you about the tello.'

'About the what?' Mum practically shrieked above the sound of Toby's crying.

'What about the cello?' I asked him.

He turned his big tearful eyes on me and I could only just make out what he was saying.

'I untied the strings and the wooden bit fell off. I didn't mean to break it . . .'

Toby got up from his chair and ran into the side of me, nearly knocking me off my own chair. He buried his head in my arm and tried to hug me awkwardly as though he couldn't bear what he'd done to me. I wanted to swallow but the lump in my throat was hurting me too much.

'But why did you touch it in the first place?' I asked him as gently as I could.

'Petronella took it out of its case after our baths. She said she was allowed, and she was showing me all about it. She said it was good for the strings to undo them till they went floppy. She said I could wind them back up tight again with the knobs at the top but the more I winded the more floppier they was . . . She just put it back in its case and said it didn't matter, because you would wind it all up in only one minute.'

His little fingers were digging into my flesh, he was clinging on so tightly. I had to put him out of his agony.

'It's all right, Toby,' I said, prising his fingers off me with one hand and stroking his hair with the other. 'It's not your fault. I'm not cross with you.'

It was as though he didn't believe me because he wouldn't let go. Meanwhile Petronella had got down from the table and was making for the door.

'Where are you off to, young lady?' said Mum, in the iciest voice I'd ever heard her use.

'To watch my programme,' said Petronella, sticking her chin up.

'Come back here this minute and sit in that chair,' said Mum in the same tone.

Petronella didn't need telling twice.

At that moment the doorbell rang. I went to answer it. It was Suzanne.

'All set, Lissie?'

Her nice bright voice filtered into our kitchen like a glimmer of sunshine over a frozen white wasteland.

'I'll just get my coat and my cello.'

'What's Leanne's surname?' Mum asked me, her voice shaking.

'Goyder,' I answered, wondering why she wanted to know.

'Don't go, Lissie,' said Toby. 'I'll never touch your tello again, honest.'

I kissed his wet cheek and assured him I wasn't going to be long and when I came back I'd give him another kiss.

He nodded sadly. Petronella stared straight ahead of her. Mum squeezed my arm and spoke in a whisper so Suzanne wouldn't hear.

'I'm sorry, love – really sorry. I'll sort it all out, don't worry. Have a good evening. We'll talk properly when you get home.' She came to the door with me. 'Thanks again, Suzanne. It's very kind of you.'

'No problem.'

When we got to the car, I turned round. Mum was still standing at the door. She raised her hand and gave me a little wave and a warm smile.

It felt as though everything inside my body had been dislodged, but it all fell back into place at that moment. I smiled back.

# 15 FIXED FOR EVER

Suzanne and Claire were both in chatty moods, which meant I could just sit there with my thoughts. It was also good that I was out of the house for the evening. If I'd had to stay in the same room as Petronella I would have killed her. I'd always known she was naughty, but I'd had no idea just how bad she really was. And as for poor little Toby... manipulated by an eight-year-old! Would Mum click that she wasn't doing the kid any favours by letting her have her own way all the time?

The school hall was packed out. I sat next to a girl called Holly, who was in the orchestra with me. Everyone who was involved in the concert was occupying the first three rows. She was in the year above me so I didn't know her all that well. I looked round and felt a sudden stab of sadness because in my daydreams up until Monday, this moment had been so very different. I'd imagined Mum and Nigel sitting near the front watching me proudly, and all my friends cheering for me from the back somewhere. In my wildest dreams Dad had even flown back from Portugal with Pauline, to surprise me. It was silly to think of all that I'd imagined, because it only made me feel more alone than ever.

I studied the programme instead. The first half of the evening was to be like an ordinary concert, including the orchestra and the choir, and the second half would consist of the four finalists and the adjudicator's comments and marks. I looked at the finalists sitting nervously in the front row to my right. One of them was talking to Mr Crane. It was Harriet Sherborne from my house. She looked upset. Mr Crane seemed to be trying to calm her down.

Usually when it's the start of a concert that I'm playing in, a lovely wave of excitement comes over me, but this evening I didn't really feel anything. It was as though my emotions had all been drained out of me, with everything that had happened in my family. Even when I played in the orchestra and sang in the choir, I didn't feel anything except a bit bored.

I was glad when the interval was over and the audience were all back in their seats.

Mr Crane came on to the stage and said he had a rather sad announcement to make. The hall went deathly quiet.

'I'm afraid there will only be three of our

four finalists playing this evening, ladies and gentlemen, because poor Harriet trapped two of her fingers in the car door, coming here tonight . . .' A gasp of sympathetic pain ran round the audience. 'We've been keeping an eye on them during the first half, but sadly they're hurting too much for Harriet to be able to apply pressure on her strings.'

From the back of the hall came a voice I recognised. It was Leanne. What on earth was she doing here? She hadn't been there during the first half.

'Lissie Raines'll take her place. She can do it.'

I turned round in disbelief at what I was hearing. Then I got an even bigger shock because Mum and Nigel were sitting next to Leanne, smiling away. And there beside them was Ollie, who gave me a thumbs-up sign. I couldn't work out where they'd all sprung from.

Another voice from the front made me turn back round again.

'Yes, Lissie, you can do it. We can't let our house down.'

It was Harriet speaking. I felt as though I was being bombarded from all angles.

'It's up to you, Lissie,' said Mr Crane, sounding a bit doubtful.

The audience was waiting for my answer. I swallowed and looked at Leanne again.

'Go on, Liss,' she said pleadingly.

Dad was the only person who ever called me Liss. It was just as though he was sitting there himself asking me to play.

'OK,' I agreed quietly, and the whole audience burst into applause.

It was probably the most nerve-racking experience of my life sitting through the three pieces that the other finalists played. They all sounded brilliant to me, and I began to think

I must have been mad to agree to play. When I got up for my turn, I heard someone near the front of the audience say, 'She's very young. Surely she's not up to it.'

That did it. I was suddenly determined to show her and everyone else that I *was* up to it. I tuned my cello carefully, then began to play my piece. The moment the first notes came off my bow I started to imagine the tropical seas. I felt as though I was actually floating on a lilo staring up at the shimmering sky. And the next thing I knew I jumped out of my skin because the audience was clapping so loudly. I stood up and saw Leanne standing up at the back. She was clapping above her head and jumping up and down. It was a good job there was no one sitting behind her! Mum and Nigel were clapping and smiling too. In fact the whole audience seemed to be smiling. I couldn't believe they were smiling at me.

I sat down in my place as the adjudicator and Mr Crane went on to the stage. Mr Crane welcomed the adjudicator, whose name was Richard Mason, and then he stood to one side to let Mr Mason give his marks.

'I have thoroughly enjoyed this evening,' began Mr Mason. 'The standard of music at this school is remarkably high and I think these four finalists are a real credit to Mr Crane and to their teachers. I'm going to give you the result straight away because I know you don't want to listen to me rambling on all night.' The audience laughed. 'I shall give the marks in the order in which the students played. Carla Briggs – 36, Tim Eccersley – 38, Anna White – 35 and Melissa Raines . . .' I'd been holding my breath so long I felt faint . . . '37.'

I sat there, while the clapping went on and on all around me. I just couldn't believe my ears! Even in my best daydreams I hadn't come second. Dad was going to be so proud of me. I couldn't wait to phone him.

The girl next to me was elbowing me. 'Go on, you've got to collect your certificate.'

I jumped to my feet, feeling silly because I hadn't realised I had to collect anything. Then with trembling legs I went up on to the stage with the others. The clapping was still as loud as ever. Mr Mason shook hands with me and handed me my certificate. I was about to leave the stage when Mr Crane stopped me.

'Melissa, you were fantastic,' he told me, patting me on the back. 'I knew you were good, but I'd no idea you were *that* good! You're going to be in everything now, you realise!' I could hardly hear him because of the clapping. 'And I'm so glad to see your cello mended. I'm afraid I never did find the culprit.'

'It's all right, *I've* found the culprit.'

He nodded and patted me on the back

again. Then I went back to my place. Mr Crane was still talking but I hardly heard a word he said I was on such a high. After another burst of applause, people started getting up to make their way home. Lots of people congratulated me as I packed away my cello, and then Mum was beside me with Nigel, Leanne and Ollie. Leanne gave me a big hug.

'I was so proud of you!' Mum said a little shakily.

'She was actually in tears,' Nigel told me with a wink.

'Oh come on, Sheila,' joked Ollie. 'She didn't play *that* badly.'

'You played out of your skin,' said Nigel. 'And Lissie,' he added, '*I'm* sorry too . . .'

I felt embarrassed that Nigel was apologising to me so I quickly changed the subject.

'I couldn't believe it when I turned round and saw you all there!'

'Your mum phoned me,' explained Leanne, 'to tell me that Crank had turned up.'

I looked at Mum questioningly.

'I've told Leanne all about it, love,' she said. 'I'm just so sorry about everything. I know now what a tough time you've been having. We'll talk later.'

'Er . . . so have you got . . . er . . .' Leanne began, sounding a bit embarrassed.

'Yeah, right,' I said, pulling Crank out of my pocket. 'He's been a lucky mascot for me tonight, but I don't need luck any more, so I expect you want him back, don't you?'

'You're not kidding!' she said, snatching him out of my hand so quickly that we all laughed.

It wasn't till we'd just dropped Leanne off at her house, and the four of us were heading for Ollie's place to drop *him* off, that I suddenly thought of something.

'Who's looking after Petronella and Toby, Mum?'

'Sally, bless her. She came round at absolutely no notice at all. The moment Nigel came in and I told him what had happened, he said, "What are we waiting for? We need to get to that concert for Lissie's sake."'

I felt so touched that Nigel had wanted to be there for me. He wasn't even my proper dad.

'Well, to be honest, Ollie phoned me at work and told me a few things, including the fact that he wanted to come along tonight,' Nigel explained.

I turned to look at Ollie. It was quite dark but I caught the wink he gave me. A few minutes later we dropped him off, having made plans for him to come over at the weekend. Nigel didn't drive off straight away. He turned to look at me, and it was as though he was finishing off what he'd just been saying.

'But you know, Lissie, I wasn't sure what to think until Sally came round this evening, and your mum told her that Petronella was in disgrace. You see, Sally asked if it was because of her torn coat. Apparently she'd actually seen Petronella doing it, but she didn't like to say anything. So when she heard that you'd taken the blame, she felt terrible and wished she'd told us earlier.'

'And we felt terrible too, love,' said Mum, turning to me with tears in her eyes. 'I'd already torn Petronella off a strip before Sal even arrived, but I went ballistic when I heard about the coat. Petronella went straight up to Sal and apologised to her.'

'Petronella apologised?' I gasped.

'She realised she'd been sussed, love – and I don't just mean about the coat or the cello or Crank – I mean about everything. In fact I have the feeling she'll be turning over a new leaf now. And so will we.' Mum's hand reached for mine in the semi-darkness. 'I'm so sorry, Lissie. I really have been blind to Petronella's bad behaviour. I've tried to excuse her, telling myself that she's only eight and she's not used to having to share me like this. But the bottom line is, Nigel and I have been spoiling her. This evening I just came to my senses and suddenly saw things from your point of view. I *am* sorry, love.'

'It's OK,' I said, because I didn't know what else to say. I felt like singing and crying at the same time.

When we went in through the front door I saw the biggest bouquet of flowers I'd ever seen on the table in the hall.

'Those are for you,' said Mum. 'They came earlier on, only I was under strict instructions not to let you see them till after the concert, so they've been in the shed!'

I opened the little envelope and read the card.

*For Liss, with all my love, from Dad, and lots of love from Pauline. Hope the evening went well. See you soon. XX*

'I can't wait to tell him what happened,' I said.

'He'll be really pleased,' said Mum.

While Mum went in to see Sally, I went upstairs. On my pillow was a large home-made card. On the front was a picture entitled MY FAMILY. In the picture there were two grown-ups, a big girl, a smaller girl, a big boy, a smaller boy and a very small boy. The big girl and the little girl were holding hands. I opened it up. Inside, in Petronella's best writing, it read:

> *Dear Lissie,*
> *I'm very very sorry I have been being a horrible girl to you when you haven't even*

*got your daddy here. I kept on wishing I*
*could play the chello like you can, but I*
*new Id never ever do it. I think I was*
*jellus, but I'v stopped now. Promis. Plees*
*give me a kiss when you come back. I will*
*be only nice from now on.*
*Love Petronella, your sister.*

When I gave her a kiss I could tell that she must have been crying and crying because her pillow was wet and her face was very hot and red. She didn't wake up, so I tiptoed out and went into Toby's room.

A little voice came out of the darkness, 'The tello didn't break again, did it?'

'No, it was perfect.'

'What if it breaks again?'

Poor Toby was still blaming himself.

'It won't break again. It's all fixed for ever.'

'Promise?'

'Promise.'

He turned over and curled right up. He could sleep peacefully now he was sure it was all fixed for ever.

And so could I.

**What happens next in the step-chain?**
**Meet Becca in**

# 1 BIG NEWS

I should have known this was going to be a bad day from the moment I got out of bed and squinted at myself in the mirror. There, shining like a beacon in the very middle of my chin was the biggest spot I've ever seen on anyone. It made the other few spots on my face look like the tiniest of freckles. I rootled around on my dressing-table desperately searching for some spot cream, then pulled the dressing-table away from the wall to see if it had fallen down the back. Big mistake! All I succeeded in doing was making the pots and sticks, jars and bottles from the top of my dressing-table go sliding off the front.

It was too dark for me to see behind, and I couldn't lug the thing any further away from the wall because my hairbrush was wedged underneath it at the front, so I crouched down and tried to squeeze myself between the back of *it* and the wall. And guess what – my head got stuck.

'You stupid, pathetic thing!' I screeched at the dressing-table. And I heard Mum's voice come floating up from the kitchen. I couldn't make out what she was saying because one of my ears was pressed against the wall and the other against the back of the dressing-table. And that just made me even madder.

Next thing, I heard her voice right behind me.

'Oh Becky, you do look funny!' she

spluttered through her giggles. 'Sorry to laugh, love . . . Are you all right?'

'No, I am *not* all right,' I snapped.

'Here, let me help.'

Mum must have unwedged my hairbrush, because the dressing-table suddenly moved with a big jolt about ten centimetres, and I managed to get my head out. She was still trying not to laugh, which made me want to kill her.

'Did you drop something down there?' she asked, struggling to keep a serious look on her face.

'No, Mum, I'm just doing my head-squeezing exercises.' That made her really crease up. '. . . and stop staring at me.'

I saw her purse her lips to try to stop herself laughing before she went out. I really didn't know what was so funny . . . until I looked in the mirror.

'Oh great!'

My ears were bright red, I'd got dust round one side of my face and a furry grey cobweb in my fringe. Didn't Mum *ever* clean behind furniture?

Mum didn't look at me when I went down for breakfast. I'd put make-up on the spot so it didn't shine so much. It just looked crusty and a bit brown. I'd done what I could with my hair, but I'm in the middle of growing it so it's not really got a style. It kind of hangs around my face in strange-looking clumps. There was no way I could make my actual body look nice because our school uniform must have been designed by a ninety-year-old man who's colour-blind and hates girls.

'Do you want me to try and do something with that spot?' Mum asked in her gentlest voice.

'You're not squeezing it, Mum.'

'I've no intention of squeezing it. I was going to re-apply the make-up, that's all.'

So she did, and I had to admit, it looked a whole lot better when she'd finished.

'We'll have a take-away tonight, shall we?' she went on brightly.

And I stopped in the middle of stuffing my packed lunch in my schoolbag. You see, I know my mum, and I knew for sure and certain that the take-away wasn't the only thing on Mum's agenda. No – she had something important that she wanted to talk to me about. Her voice was too bright. She didn't fool me for a minute.

'Why? What have you got to tell me?' I asked, narrowing my eyes.

'Well, we'll talk later shall we . . . over the take-away?'

'*She's* nice.'

'She's *lovely*!'

'*She's* wearing those trousers my sister wants . . .'

'You're very quiet, Bex,' commented Louise.

'Mmm.'

I've tried hard to train people to call me Becca, but no one takes any notice of me. It's always Becky from Mum, Gran and my teachers, and Bex from my friends.

'Is something wrong?' asked Maddy.

'Probably not.'

I picked up a piece of my hair and inspected it for split ends. Even without looking at the others I knew I'd got them interested.

'Oh come on, stop being mysterious, Bex,' said Tanya. 'We're all dying to know what's up now.'

They all leaned forwards as though I was about to let them in on something juicy I'd found out about one of the teachers or something.

'You know Mum . . .'

'Yeah, she's got that boyfriend, hasn't she?'

'And they've just got back from Portugal, haven't they?'

'She's not dumped him, has she?'

'Omigod!' screeched Maddy. 'Don't say *he's* dumped *her*! That's it, isn't it, Bex?'

'Or are they getting married or something?' squeaked Tanya.

'Yeah, and he's got a job as a missionary in Africa and you've got to go and live in a mud hut . . .' Louise finished off, eyes wide.

'Look, do you want to know, or what?' I said in my best nanny's voice to shut them up.

'Yeah . . . sorry.'

They waited, all big eyed and excited, and I suddenly realised I didn't actually have anything to tell them. I mean, they weren't going to be too impressed with the truth . . .

*Mum's going to talk to me this evening.*

*What about?*

*Dunno.*

I had to say it though. They were all waiting breathlessly.

'Well, you know Mum . . .' I was speaking really slowly, desperately hoping that I might suddenly think of a way of making my great non-event sound like something stunningly mysterious. It was no good. I'd just have to say it. 'Well she wants to talk to me about something and I don't know what it is . . .'

Tanya looked puzzled. 'So what makes you think it might be something important?'

'Just a feeling,' I said, trying to look mysterious.

Louise giggled. 'You do look funny when you squint like that, Bex.'

(That's the last time I'll try to look mysterious.)

Maddy put her arm round me. 'Don't be horrible, Lou. Bex might be about to have a baby sister or something, you never know.'

'Cool!' said Tanya.

Then they all went back to the magazine. Just like that! Leaving me with my jaw dropped open, contemplating a baby sister or brother.

While Mum was picking up the take-away that evening, and I was at home getting plates and knives and forks out, I started day-dreaming.

*What did your mum say, Bex?*

*Oh, nothing much – just that when she was in Portugal she bought a lottery ticket and she won, so we're buying a villa out there . . . Yeah, cool, isn't it? Mum's just picking up the Porsche at the moment . . . What? No, she's given up work for ever . . . Sorry, can't make it after school . . . we're popping over to Paris for dinner . . .*

I was so deep in my dream, I didn't hear Mum coming in.

A couple of minutes later we were tucking into chicken korma and all the trimmings. Mum was blinking rapidly, like she always does when she's concentrating or nervous. The moment had come.

'You haven't got any sleepovers or anything planned for Saturday evening, have you?' she began, her eyes on the korma, her voice trying to sound casual.

My heartbeat went up a bit. 'No . . .'

'Only I was going to invite Patrick over . . .'

So? Nothing unusual about that.

'Uh-huh . . .'

'And there's someone he wants you to meet . . .'

My heart rate doubled. And my mind went into overdrive. *Patrick was gay. He was bringing his partner along. Mum isn't going out with*

*Patrick at all. I'd got it all wrong.* What would my friends make of *this*!

'. . . And *she* wants to meet *you*, too,' Mum went on, smiling shakily.

'*She*?'

'Who?'

'Patrick's daughter . . . Lissie . . . She's thirteen . . . just like you.'

# Collect the links in the step-chain . . .

1. To see her dad Sarah has to stay with the woman who wrecked her family. Will she do it? Find out in *One Mum Too Many*

2. Ollie thinks a holiday with girls will be a nightmare. And it is, because he's fallen for his stepsister. Can it get any worse? Find out in *You Can't Fancy Your Stepsister*

4. Becca's mum describes her boyfriend's daughter as perfect in every way. Can Becca

bear to meet her? Find out in *Too Good To Be True*

5. Ed's stepsisters are getting seriously on his nerves. Should he go and live with his mum? Find out in *Get Me Out Of Here*

6. Hannah and Rachel are stepsisters. They're also best friends. What will happen to them if their parents split up? Find out in *Parents Behaving Badly*